THE GOLDEN RULE

NewCon Press Novellas

Set 1: Science Fiction (Cover art by Chris Moore)
The Iron Tactician – Alastair Reynolds
At the Speed of Light – Simon Morden
The Enclave – Anne Charnock
The Memoirist – Neil Williamson

Set 2: Dark Thrillers (Cover art by Vincent Sammy)
Sherlock Holmes: Case of the Bedevilled Poet – Simon Clark
Cottingley – Alison Littlewood
The Body in the Woods – Sarah Lotz
The Wind – Jay Caselberg

Set 3: The Martian Quartet (Cover art by Jim Burns)
The Martian Job – Jaine Fenn
Sherlock Holmes: The Martian Simulacra – Eric Brown
Phosphorous: A Winterstrike Story – Liz Williams
The Greatest Story Ever Told – Una McCormack

Set 4: Strange Tales (Cover art by Ben Baldwin)
Ghost Frequencies – Gary Gibson
The Lake Boy – Adam Roberts
Matryoshka – Ricardo Pinto
The Land of Somewhere Safe – Hal Duncan

Set 5: The Alien Among Us (Cover art by Peter Hollinghurst)
Nomads – Dave Hutchinson
Morpho – Philip Palmer
The Man Who Would be Kling – Adam Roberts
Macsen Against the Jugger – Simon Morden

Set 6: Blood and Blade (Cover art by Duncan Kay)
The Bone Shaker – Edward Cox
A Hazardous Engagement – Gaie Sebold
Serpent Rose – Kari Sperring
Chivalry – Gavin Smith

Set 7: Robot Dreams (Cover art by Fangorn)
According To Kovac – Andrew Bannister
Deep Learning – Ren Warom
Paper Hearts – Justina Robson
The Beasts Of Lake Oph – Tom Toner

THE GOLDEN RULE

Juliet E. McKenna

NewCon Press
England

First published in the UK by NewCon Press
41 Wheatsheaf Road, Alconbury Weston, Cambs, PE28 4LF
September 2022

NCP287 (limited edition hardback)
NCP288 (softback)

10 9 8 7 6 5 4 3 2 1

ISBN:

978-1-914953-32-3 (hardback)
978-1-914953-33-0 (softback)

Cover art and front cover graphics by Justin Tan
Back cover layout by Ian Whates

Editorial meddling by Ian Whates
Typesetting by Ian Whates

ONE

'Wake up, Davey boy!' A fist hammered on his door as heavy boots clumped along the landing. The men coming off shift were arriving back at the tenement.

'I'm up, you arsehole,' he called back without rancour. In fact, he was already shaved, dressed and ready to leave. He had also slept fairly well. One advantage of working nights was he got this room to himself in the mornings, while the other constables he shared with were out pounding their beats. The noise from the streets outside leading down to East London's docks was far easier to ignore than three men in beds crammed together snoring, farting and mumbling in their sleep.

He checked his boots, his uniform trousers and his tunic. His buttons were polished and his newly issued whistle was secure on its chain. He'd heard those were soon going to be issued to all police officers, now they had proved so much easier to hear than an old-fashioned watchman's rattle. He secured his broad leather belt with its gleaming snake buckle and checked that his lantern was clipped on tight – and that the blasted lamp wasn't leaking oil. He slipped his lancewood truncheon into its special pocket on his trouser leg and picked up his tightly rolled waterproof cape. David secured that to his belt with its ties.

Not that there was much danger of rain as this hot, dry May turned to June, but every young constable soon learned their rolled cape was just as useful as their truncheon when they needed a weapon. More useful sometimes, if you wanted to give some scoundrel a beating without leaving too many obvious marks, just to make him think twice about whatever villainy he might be contemplating. Last of all, he picked up his tall helmet, grateful as always for the inches it added to his modest height.

Satisfied that he'd pass muster on parade at the station, David headed downstairs to the kitchen. The sergeant's wife was peeling potatoes at the sink. He saw she had a thick slice of bread and dripping waiting for him, along with a mug of strong, sweet tea.

'Good evening, Mrs Shaw,' he said politely.

'Good evening, Constable Price.' She gestured at the table. 'There you go.'

'Thank you.' David sat down to eat his breakfast.

Other young constables came and went around him, all equally respectful towards the short, stout woman in her long brown dress and spotless white apron. Mrs Shaw ran this barracks for unmarried police officers with a rod of iron, and woe betide any raw recruit who thought he could treat her like some skivvy.

'Thank you.' David said again, as he stood up and checked his tunic for crumbs.

Mrs Shaw nodded. 'Your dinner'll be warm on the 'ot plate when you get in. I got a nice bit of ox liver for you boys tonight.'

'Thank you.' David reckoned a slab of liver would be leathery enough to resole his boots after hours sitting under an upturned plate on the back of the kitchen range. Still, he'd be hungry enough to eat it and the mash and cabbage couldn't come to too much harm.

He headed out and walked the short distance to the station. The streets were still busy even though the sun was sinking, and not just with working men. The light lingered on these long summer evenings, drawing the locals out of doors. David could hardly blame them for preferring a chat and a drink with their neighbours out on the cobbles, rather than staying in their cramped and stuffy rooms. There were more people than ever crammed into these tall, soot-stained brick buildings. The great procession to celebrate Queen Victoria's Golden Jubilee in this Year of Our Lord 1887 was only a few weeks away. Every family in the district seemed to have invited their relatives to come and stay for the whole month.

David wondered how many people would actually make the trek from the docks to see the queen in her carriage as she travelled from Buckingham Palace to Westminster Abbey. How many more would seize the excuse to spend the day downing pint after pint in the local pubs? Midsummer's Day wouldn't be any sort of holiday for him and his colleagues, as they were called on to break up drunken fights, and to remonstrate with belligerent husbands when some unfortunate woman's screams got too loud for the neighbours to stand.

There was the usual crowd around the steps to the police station, to report people or property lost, stolen or strayed. David walked past them, and past those already inside waiting to unload their woes on the officer at the front counter.

Sergeant Shaw was standing at the lectern in the day room. As David entered, he looked up and quickly folded whatever he had been reading. He nodded as he tucked the sheet of paper into a tunic pocket. 'First one here again, Price. Good lad.'

'Thank you, Sergeant.' David dutifully ducked his head.

The other constables were already filing in. Each one breathed more easily once the sergeant acknowledged them. That meant they had passed his eagle-eyed inspection. Once every name had been ticked off in the ledger, Sergeant Shaw set down his pen and addressed the parade.

'It's the start of the month, so that means rent's due and we all know there'll be some as can't pay. If I catch any of you turning a blind eye to some family trying a moonlight flit, I'll have your guts for garters. Never mind the sob stories, we've heard 'em all and precious few are true. This 'ot weather, there'll be windows left open and forgotten about, and it's our duty to see all premises made secure. Make sure you do, and never mind if you get an earful because you've woke somebody up. That just means they'll be more careful next time.'

He scowled. 'Billy Cameron's back on the streets, and there's been word Alfie Brown's come 'ome. You see either of them out and about, you ask them their business, and you get the names of whoever's loitering with the bastards. Then you send them on their way because they'll be up to no good, I'll be bound. Right, that's your lot. Get going.'

David followed the rest of the constables as they filed out of the day room and through the station onto the streets. Some turned right, others turned left. David headed towards the river with a dozen others. As they made their way through the tangle of narrow lanes, men headed off at every junction. Finally David was walking on his own, along the beat that was so familiar now he reckoned he could walk it blindfold.

The tide was going out, and the rank smell of Thames mud floated over the reek of the filth in the gutters. The river might not be the stream of shit and worse that the constables born and bred in London remembered from their childhoods, but newcomers to the city like David still reckoned the water was pretty foul.

He had got used to the smell by now. He walked along the empty street at the regulation pace that recruits soon learned; two and a half miles an hour. His allotted circuit was mostly shops and warehouses and there was no one around so late. All the same, David made sure to try every doorknob and handle as he passed. If some unlocked premises was found to be robbed in the morning, that beat's constable would face a hefty fine at best, and dismissal at worst.

He whistled cheerily as he turned the next corner. This particular street had deep-set doorways and was close enough to the river for the whores to bring their customers here to find what passed for privacy. Sure enough, he saw a couple of shadowy figures hurry out of a dim recess and head in the opposite direction. That saved David an argument with some man who didn't see why he shouldn't take his pleasure when and where he wanted. Add to that, a night in the cells and a summons for soliciting wouldn't do anything to improve the life of a wretched girl reduced to selling herself.

He completed his first patrol without incident and turned the final corner where he expected to see Constable Thompson waiting. Jimmy was always the first one to reach this intersection of their beats, where a brief conversation confirmed that neither of them had been hit over the head or succumbed to the temptation of a doze in a doorway.

Jimmy was there, but he wasn't alone. As David got closer, he saw Sergeant Shaw. David's heart sank. He'd told Jimmy time and again that he needed to be thorough with his checks. A feckless constable might be fined and dismissed, but the sergeant responsible for him faced demotion. That would have dire consequences for his family once they were turned out of police married quarters. No wonder sergeants regularly slipped out of the station to assess constables they suspected weren't up to snuff. Though as David got closer still, he saw a handful of other constables were there too.

'Sarge?' He spoke as soon as he was near enough not to have to raise his voice. 'Is there some trouble?'

Shaw scowled. 'Bloody Lascars, fighting each other down at that 'ostel that's been opened for them. Only to be expected from a bunch of 'eathens and thieves jumping ship the first chance they get. You 'ave your truncheons ready, lads.' He addressed the whole group. 'They'll all 'ave knives, the vicious scum, so you go in 'ard and don't bother asking questions because they won't 'ardly none of them speak the Queen's English, and them as does will just tell you lies.'

Shaw was already walking away. The constables followed obediently. Shaw continued his warnings about the threats that these Lascars posed, not merely to the stalwart policemen who would be forced to subdue them, but to good Christian men and women who had the misfortune to cross their paths. Especially women. Shaw hinted darkly at unnatural lusts leading to unspecified outrages.

David was puzzled. From the way the sergeant was talking, it seemed these unspeakable crimes were a daily occurrence, but he couldn't recall any recent reports at parade, or even gossip back at the barracks. Obviously he encountered Lascars himself from time to time, mostly idle beggars who needed moving on, but they showed his uniform the proper respect, or were incapable of causing trouble as a consequence of the opium they had been smoking. That really was a filthy habit, and David objected to the notion of hard-working men's charitable pennies paying for such a vice, but evidently such heathens knew no better, or had no shame.

He dismissed such thoughts as their route reached the broad road where the new hostel had recently been opened in a refurbished warehouse. A lamp over the entrance illuminated the words freshly carved into the stone lintel. *Society for the Relief of Asiatic Seafarers.*

Sergeant Shaw muttered something David was pretty sure was disobliging, if not downright obscene. Since the last word was definitely 'do-gooders' he didn't ask the sergeant to repeat himself. Besides, he was rather more concerned at the size of the gathering on the street by the hostel door. A substantial crowd was clearly visible in the golden glow of the street lights.

'They ain't Lascars, Sarge,' a voice that David didn't recognise said doubtfully.

Whoever was speaking, they were right. Even at this distance, the constables could see these were men of far darker complexion and greater stature than the lithe sailors who hailed from the Empire's Indian shores.

'They ain't fighting neither,' another constable observed practically.

There was no denying it. The Africans were standing in peaceful groups, laughing and chatting. A match flared as one offered another a light. Cigarette and pipe smoke drifted towards the policemen on the gentle breeze.

Swift footsteps behind them echoed back from the tall warehouse walls. Sergeant Shaw whirled around, with his truncheon raised. David saw a column of indistinct figures cross from one side of the street to another, cutting through the alleys that ran behind the buildings.

'Right, lads, here we go.' The sergeant held his truncheon high, but there was an odd tremor in his voice.

Before David could decide what that might mean, the trotting figures disappeared. What on earth was going on?

A few moments later, Jimmy Thompson echoed his confusion. 'What's all this then? Chinamen?'

They saw the newcomers they had glimpsed emerge from the alley opposite the hostel door. There were a considerable number of them, and the street lights clearly showed they hailed from further east than India's fabled shores. Some wore the distinctive garb of their homeland with long plaited hair down their backs, while the rest were dressed like any other man who worked along the river. Some looked respectable enough to be clerks or secretaries working for the city's merchants.

The Africans turned as they saw the newcomers. David's hand strayed towards his truncheon. The wooden weapon stayed in its pocket. There was no sign of any confrontation. Far from it. The Africans greeted their Oriental brethren with hearty good cheer. Those conversational circles widened to admit newcomers and cigarettes were exchanged.

'Sarge?'

Sharing Jimmy's bafflement, David saw that Shaw was equally bemused. Though that wasn't the only emotion on his face... Before he could make any guess at the sergeant's thoughts, hobnailed boots clattered on the cobbles.

A gang of youths appeared from a side street that must run parallel to the one the police had followed to get here. As they spilled out onto the main thoroughfare, the mob began jeering and whistling. There could be no doubt as to their target, and the menace in their voices was clear, in sharp contrast to the good humour of the crowd outside the hostel. Their Cockney accents were equally unmistakable, along with the pallor of their spiteful faces.

The Africans and the Chinamen fell silent. Cigarettes were dropped and stamped out as they turned to face the approaching louts. Looking from one side to the other, David saw the glint of steel here and there, but not in the hands of those standing in the lamplight. This mob of home-grown ruffians were the ones who had come armed for a fight. David could see a good few carried pick axe handles or wooden barrel staves that would serve just as well for cracking skulls. They hadn't only come here prepared to fight, he realised. They were intent on provoking trouble.

'Time to keep the peace, lads,' Harry Simmonds said cheerfully. He held his whistle ready to blow and prepared to step out into the main road.

'Wait!' Shaw said.

The other constables were ready to follow Simmonds, truncheons in hand. They looked at the sergeant, confused. Why delay? As soon as they advanced, the policemen would be standing between the suspicious but undeniably peaceable gathering outside the hostel and this belligerent gang. Their whistles would summon more constables from all directions. That would surely prevent any violence.

David couldn't deny that the Londoners were the greater threat to good order tonight. He searched the faces of the front rank as they approached for any sign of a leader. Take the key man down fast and hard, and that would break the spirit of most of the others.

It was already apparent that the gang's bravado was fading. They might not have glimpsed the constables – who were still obediently holding back, however puzzled they might be – but the louts could clearly see they were significantly outnumbered by the Africans and the Chinamen. A moment later, the door to the hostel opened. A cohort of Lascars emerged, dark-skinned and wearing the shapeless and coarse cotton clothing that was far more suited to the latitudes where they had signed on to serve the Empire's merchant ships.

The last of the jeers from the approaching mob died away, uncertain. David saw those in the front rank glance at each other. They were waiting for someone else to make a decision. Then he saw one of them look straight at the side street where the policemen were still waiting.

Was he expecting reinforcements? Had another gang arrived behind them unnoticed? David snatched a glance over his shoulder. In that instant, he saw two things. The street behind them was empty, and Sergeant Shaw was absolutely furious. How peculiar.

'Don't fancy your chances now, do you?' Harry Simmonds mocked, though the mob was out of earshot. 'Not so brave when it's four to one against you?'

The gang was retreating, slowly at first and then scattering more quickly. Barely a handful lingered. One of them was the man who had looked in their direction. He did that a second time, and this time he nodded. David was certain of it.

A moment later, Sergeant Shaw spoke. 'Looks like that's over then, and no harm done. Best get back to your beats, boys, and make damn sure there's been no mischief while you was elsewhere.'

'You think that's what this was about, Sarge?' somebody asked, alarmed.

'Could very well be,' Shaw said quickly. 'Someone starting a rumour to see who gets pulled off what beat. So keep this to yourselves, lads, even around the station. We don't want to give anything away, and we don't want to give anyone any bright ideas. Do you hear me?'

'Yes, Sarge,' the constables chorused.

David added his voice to the rest, and the others went their separate ways. As he walked away with Jimmy Thompson, though, he grew more and more uneasy. Of course it was possible that someone had been inspired to draw some of the district's constables off their beats with a pack of convincing lies, but how likely was it that they would back up their subterfuge by sending a gang to attack the Lascars' hostel?

On the one hand, he was forced to admit, there were plenty of riff-raff born and bred around the docks who had no love for the police. Boys from families who preferred to live by theft, brutality and trickery instead of honest hard work. David reckoned a good many of them could be persuaded to make a nuisance of themselves, especially if that offered the chance of getting a few blows in by way of revenge for a childhood of clips around the ear from some constable still hoping to drive such urchins back towards the straight and narrow.

On the other hand, the Londoners hadn't attacked the police. Their target had undeniably been the Asiatic Seafarers' hostel. The vile insults and epithets the mob had been hurling made that clear as day. The gang had only backed down when they saw how badly they were outnumbered.

Then there was the puzzle of the motley force gathered to defend the hostel. They might not have been armed, and thus liable to face awkward questions from the police, but it would have been the work of moments for them to retrieve clubs or knives dropped to the ground by their enemies. They were well used to wielding such weapons in their violent homelands, from what David had heard.

But who could have got word to so many different men of so many different races? Word that would be believed. How could that be in service of some plan to draw police constables off their beats, especially when there could be no way to know which constables would be summoned? The more David thought about such a convoluted scheme, the more unlikely he found the idea.

Even so, he made a thorough check of every door and window as he started on the next circuit of his beat. David might not believe in conspiracies, but some opportunist could always have noticed his absence and seized this chance for a spot of housebreaking.

His route took him closer and closer to the Thames. He came out of an alley onto the quayside. Gas lamps on the far bank were glinting on the water and while there was no moon, the cloudless summer sky offered him starlight to see by, when he heard running feet.

Three figures were running towards him; two clearly chasing the one in the lead. The first man passed under a street light and David saw his dark skin. Was he one of the Africans who had gathered outside the Lascar hostel or had he committed some crime? Either way, he would soon outstrip his pursuers.

Just as David decided he had a duty to stop the fugitive and get some answers, the dark-skinned man saw the constable. He skidded to a halt.

'You wait there!' David drew his truncheon to defend himself as he hurried towards the man.

The African took long strides towards the river. He was rummaging in his jacket pocket. David caught a glimpse of something small as the man hurled it as far as he could over the water.

That delay cost the dark-skinned man dearly. The pair hunting him had got between him and any hope of escape, keeping him with his back to the river. They spread out, not far enough apart to allow him to slip between them, and David could see they were both carrying clubs. They advanced towards their quarry. The African looked from side to side. He spread his hands wide, and David saw he was unarmed. Thief he might well be, but he should face justice before a magistrate, not at the hands of two dockside brutes.

'You there! Stop!' David broke into a run. His free hand groped for the chain that secured his whistle.

The hunters were momentarily distracted, looking to see who had just hailed them. The African seized his chance, trying to dart away to his left, to get away from his pursuers and David both. Luck wasn't on his side. The closest hunter sprang at him. The man used his club on the back of the African's thighs with a deftness that suggested long practise. The African went sprawling onto the quayside. Both hunters were on him now, kicking as they raised their clubs, ready to bring their wooden cudgels down with murderous intent.

'Police!' David bellowed. 'Stop! Police!'

He blew a shrill blast on his whistle, and tried to picture the routes that the closest constables would take to get here. He only hoped help wasn't too far away.

The attackers froze. They looked around. Seeing David running towards them, they hared off in the opposite direction. The constable made a swift decision not to pursue them. The brutes had let their clubs clatter to the ground, but without reinforcements he could still end up in real trouble if both men turned on him.

He slowed to a walk as he approached the African. The man lay ominously still. David saw he had curled up to protect his belly and balls from his attackers' brutal boots. He had wrapped his arms around his head to save his skull from their clubs. Had that been enough? David really hoped the man wasn't dead. He hadn't had much to do with the detective branch, who would be sent to investigate if this proved to be a murder, but he'd heard often enough that they assumed every constable was little more than a halfwit. He wouldn't do that, when he joined their ranks.

'How badly are you hurt? Do you speak English?' he asked belatedly.

The man groaned. So at least he wasn't dead, but David wasn't about to breathe easy. Plenty of men succumbed to a beating days after the fact.

The man suddenly scrambled to his feet. He darted away, leaving the constable completely flat-footed. The African vanished into the shadows before David could decide what to do. Whoever he was, he knew this stretch of the docks.

'Not that badly hurt then,' David said aloud.

A moment later, unexpected anger seized him. What on Earth was going on tonight? This must have something to do with the mysterious events at the hostel, surely? But how would he ever prove that, and what good would it do if he could?

Would whatever the dark-skinned man had thrown away offer him a clue? David spun around to look at the river. It had to have some significance. The man must have known he would be caught if he stopped to get rid of it. If he would rather take a beating than be caught in possession of – what?

David tried to picture what he had seen. The mysterious object had been small enough to be cupped in the African's hand. It had been fairly heavy, the constable realised, recalling the way it had fallen through the air. Heavy enough to fall short of the water at the current low ebb.

He was already walking towards the quayside. He reached the edge and looked down. The mud lay exposed, glistening in the starlight. He could make out darker shapes scattered along the foreshore, but there was no saying what they might be. David looked from side to side. There were ladders here and there along the dock. Urchins and vagrants used them to get down to the water's edge, to go scavenging for things they could sell to buy bread or gin. If he didn't at least try to find whatever it was, it would be lost for ever, either to the returning tide, or to some mudlark.

He put his truncheon back in its pocket, made his way to the closest ladder, and climbed cautiously down. As he reached the bottom rungs, he tested his footing. The foreshore seemed firm enough, but he still moved with slow and deliberate caution. Going back to the constables' tenement with stinking river mud staining his uniform didn't bear thinking about. He'd never hear the last of that from Mrs Shaw. As it was, he'd have to scour his boots clean at the station before he set foot over her threshold again.

Looking down, he walked towards the area where he reckoned whatever-it-was might have landed. His boots knocked against pebbles and oddments. There was no telling what they were in the gloom. David rummaged in a pocket for his safety matches. Striking a light, he reached for the lamp clipped to his belt and opened it up to light the wick. He secured the catch and unhooked the lamp to shine the beam focused by the bullseye glass on the mud at his feet. Stooping, he could see shards of muddy pottery and a dead rat.

Straightening up, he moved on. As he did so, he slipped just a little, and the toe of his boot nudged the drowned rat. David looked down. That seemed oddly solid for a dead rodent. More than that, there hadn't been any sort of squelch. Even over the low murmur of the river, David had distinctly heard a click.

Hunkering down with agonising care so as not to lose his balance, he took a closer look. That confused him even more. This was no rat, at least, not a real one. The thing's eyes were button-bright like enamel and the gaping mouth showed a strip of painted wood for teeth. Its belly had split open, but rather than a spill of guts, David saw a collection of cogwheels, as small as the inner workings of a pocket watch. There was also a scatter of tiny white squares half in and half out of the torn fur.

David had never seen anything like it. After a few moments thought, he reckoned it had to be some sort of automaton. What an African had been doing with such a fine piece of workmanship was a mystery. Not that there was a law against such things, not as far as David was aware. Had the men chasing the African known he had this? Had they wanted to get it off him? These were more questions the constable couldn't answer. Or had they just wanted to give a black man a beating after the fight they'd been eager for earlier hadn't materialised?

Could this mysterious contrivance lead him to any answers? David had absolutely no idea how he might find out more about the artificial rodent, but he wasn't going to leave it here to be washed away by the incoming tide. He set down his lamp and fished out his handkerchief. Trying not to get too much mud on the cheap cotton or on his fingers, he gathered up the clockwork rat.

'Davey! Davey-boy! What you doing down there?'

He looked up to see Jimmy Thompson looking down from the quay's edge, with Edwin Smith at his side.

'We heard your whistle. Thought you was in trouble.'

'I thought I was in for a right kicking.' David hastily shoved the damp bundle into his tunic pocket and picked up his lamp. 'Let me get back up there and I'll tell you about it.'

He quenched the wick and clipped the lamp back on his belt. Still careful, he walked back across the mud to the ladder and climbed up.

At the top, Jimmy offered him a hand. 'What's been going on then?'

Once he had both boots on the dock, David started to explain how the African had been chased along the quayside. Before he could tell Jimmy about the man stopping to throw something away, Edwin Smith spat on the ground.

'Black bastards. They need to know their place, and it sure as shit ain't here.'

David continued as if Ed hadn't spoken. 'They caught up with him and laid into him something dreadful. That's when I blew my whistle, in case they thought they could give me some of the same. That made them take to their heels, thank God, and the black man went on his way.'

Not telling the whole truth wasn't the same as lying, was it? David thrust away a recollection of Sunday School at chapel back home, where he rather thought Mrs Williams had said different.

'Up to no good, I'll be bound.' Ed scowled.

David heard the echo of Sergeant Shaw's words at this evening's parade. He remembered how often he saw Ed at the sergeant's elbow, ready to run his errands. More than one constable suspected Ed of telling tales. David also remembered the look the sergeant had exchanged with the leader of tonight's mob.

'But what was you doing down by the river?' Jimmy was puzzled.

'Thought I heard something.' David shrugged.

'Another sack of kittens?' Ed laughed unpleasantly.

'Sod you,' Jimmy said, before David could respond. 'There's no call to drown the poor little mites, not with the rats and mice what wants catching around here. Davey found homes for them, didn't he?'

David shot Jimmy a glance that told him to leave it. 'You should get back to your own beats, both of you. I'll see you back at the station.'

Ed nodded and walked away without a backward glance. Without anything out of the ordinary to tell the sergeant, David thought. He was more convinced than ever that something very odd was going on. Until he knew more, he would keep his own counsel.

Jimmy grinned. 'Better be on my way. Glad I didn't find you picking up your teeth to take home in a bag.'

'You and me both,' David said fervently.

They walked away from the river together. David listened with half an ear as Jimmy gave him chapter and verse on the doors he'd been checking on his own beat, thankfully finding nothing amiss.

'Same hereabouts.' David didn't go into details. He could feel the solid weight of the rat automaton in his tunic pocket, and was grateful that the darkness hid the bulge from Jimmy.

They reached the corner where their beats overlapped and went their separate ways. David racked his brains for a quiet corner where he might be able to examine the clockwork rat more closely. He could hardly stand underneath the gas lamp on some street corner. Unfortunately, he couldn't think of a single spot where there wasn't some chance of interruption. Besides, he was reluctantly forced to conclude, he'd need a damn sight more light than his police issue oil lamp could offer.

He would find more illumination at the station of course, but he'd have no hope of privacy there. Someone with more rank would carry the rat away, and that would be the last he'd ever see of it. How about the constables' lodgings? The thought of Mrs Shaw's reaction if he unwrapped the filthy thing on her mercilessly scrubbed kitchen table made him grin for a moment. His smile faded just as fast. Sergeant Shaw would hear about such an outrage against cleanliness and probably godliness as soon as he came home. That thought made David uneasy, even if he still had no idea why.

By the time he'd walked another round of the familiar streets, he was forced to conclude he would have to see what he could learn in the daylight coming through the window of the bedroom he shared. So he would have to stay awake until the day shift lads had gone on their way. That was going to be a challenge. And now he was thinking about that, he felt bone weary. David yawned as he rounded a corner.

'Oh!' He pulled up short to avoid walking straight into a slender figure standing there.

Standing there waiting, he realised. Waiting for him. Not waiting alone, which was only wise given she was even shorter than David. He could see two more figures standing a short distance down the street. Much taller and broader shouldered, in long overcoats despite the balmy summer night, the men had their heads together in conversation. Hearing David's exclamation, they turned to look at him.

'Good evening, Constable Price.' The lady he had nearly walked into greeted him, perfectly composed. 'Or perhaps it should be good morning, at this hour.'

'Good – day to you, madam.' Thoroughly confused, David sketched a salute, just to be on the safe side.

Whoever this slip of a girl might be, she was definitely a lady. Her impeccably educated tone made that clear. So did the delightful, flowery scent that momentarily rose above the odours of the gutter as she tucked a pale handkerchief into her cuff. He'd wager a penny to a pound that a bottle of that eau de toilette cost more than he earned in a week. A street light on the corner opposite showed him the sheen of silk on her feathered hat and that well-tailored coat must surely cover an equally expensive dress. Not that David knew much about such folderols, but the girl he was walking out with pored over the fashion plates in the illustrated papers. A man couldn't help seeing a few things.

What this well-bred lady was doing down here wasn't the biggest puzzle. The lamplight showed her complexion to be a warm brown, while her eyes were as dark as the raven tresses piled high beneath her bonnet. Her accent might be that of society's highest circles, but her ancestors had come from some far distant shore.

David realised she was smiling at him, and that she was very well aware of his scrutiny. He felt his face redden with embarrassment. 'I – that is to say...'

'You have something that belongs to me, Constable Price. You retrieved it from the riverside.' The mysterious lady held out a gloved hand. 'Be so kind as to return my property.'

'What – what is it?' David bit back a torrent of other questions.

'A child's clockwork toy, a rat,' she said blandly. 'An amusing trifle some six inches long and made with brown musquash fur.' She extended her hand an inch or so further. 'If you please.'

'How – then – why –' David folded his arms stubbornly. 'If you come to the station, and you can prove it belongs to you, well then, you can collect it from the lost property office.'

And he'd get some answers, one way or the other.

The lady's hand didn't waver and neither did her voice. 'It was not lost, merely discarded in error.'

'I saw it thrown away,' David retorted. 'That was no mistake, and nor was the beating those other two ruffians were ready to give the –' he hastily swallowed the uncouth epithet on the tip of his tongue '– the man who had it.'

'Thanks to you, no lasting harm was done.' The lady's smile was growing fixed. 'Now, Constable Price, if you will be so kind as to return –'

'How do you know who I am?' he demanded. 'Who are you, come to that?'

His frustration rang out, harsh in the silence. The two men further down the road immediately started walking towards him. He saw they were both Africans, and at least a head taller than he was. He wondered uneasily what they might be carrying underneath those overcoats. Spears?

The lady raised her hand. The two men halted.

'Your division letter and warrant number are on your collar,' she said coldly. 'As for my name, that is none of your concern. You should be thinking rather more about the consequences of being so disobliging, when you consider that I can send a telegram to learn everything I wish about you in the middle of the night. A word from me in certain quarters would do your prospects no good at all. My favour on the other hand –'

'I don't take bribes,' David said crossly, 'and I don't give in when I'm threatened neither.'

Even so, he reached into his tunic pocket. Frustrating though it was, he saw no reason to doubt this was the lady's property. She knew what he had found without any need to see it. It was equally clear that making her collect it from the station in the morning could cause him untold trouble. Whatever was going on, it couldn't be worth ending his career barely three years after he had come to London. Not for the sake of some clockwork curio.

He handed over the cloth-wrapped lump. The lady took it without any apparent concern for the river mud and water staining her pale kidskin gloves.

'Thank you.' She smiled sweetly at him.

'Save it.' He didn't care if he sounded rude.

The lady was unperturbed. 'Good night, Constable Price.' She turned and joined her bodyguards. The three of them walked away.

David drew a deep breath, and his cheeks puffed out as he let it go. What else could he have done? He watched the mysterious trio until they were out of sight. Then he resumed his patrol. What else could he do?

The rest of his shift passed without incident. He took his break and the day room was peaceful enough as he ate his meat pie and drank a mug of coffee. He went back out on his beat, and the night brought nothing more to report than a couple of drunks who needed moving along. As the sky paled, David began knocking on those doors where rousing the working men within earned him a grateful penny a week from their pay. At long last, he headed back to the station to find Sergeant Shaw in the day room.

'Anything to report?' Shaw stood at his lectern, pen poised over the ledger.

'Nothing, Sarge,' David said shortly.

It wasn't as if he had any proof of anything that had happened. The damp patch on his tunic had already dried in the warm summer night. Even the river mud on his boots had flaked off as he'd pounded the pavements. Whatever had been going on, it was over as far as Constable David Price was concerned.

TWO

Mildred liked to call herself a housemaid, but as far as David was concerned she was a maid of all work. He didn't mind her harmless little vanity. What was far more important was she worked for a decent family who treated her well. Her employer was some sort of customs officer, and his wife was originally from Kent. She was taking the sea air in Broadstairs at the moment with their three little ones. That meant Mildred was having an easy time of it, along with Mrs Jessop, the rotund and amiable cook.

She had a half day on his next day off. When David knocked on the tradesman's entrance, and she led him in past the scullery, he saw the two of them had been sitting at the kitchen table to enjoy the latest illustrated papers. With the missus away, they didn't have to wait for the last week's editions to be brought down from the drawing room.

'I'll be with you in two ticks.'

As Mildred headed up the back stairs to her attic room, Mrs Jessop looked up and smiled.

'Take the weight off while you're waiting, lad. I never knew a constable who didn't have trouble with his feet in later life.'

'Thank you.' David pulled out a chair. 'What's the latest news up in town then?'

Mrs Jessop pushed a spread of pictures towards him. 'All the foreign nobilities arriving for the Jubilee. Not just from Europe, neither. There's any number come from India, and they say there'll be a queen from Ha-why-eye. That's on the other side of the world.'

'Fancy that.' David drew the paper towards him, to look at the photographs. There was a tremendous array of royal personages as he turned the pages. Men and women alike were dressed in the height of fashion, apart from those men who had opted for military uniforms bedecked with gold braid and medals. Some of the visitors from the Empire wore what David guessed would be called 'native dress', all long robes and wide sashes like something on the music hall stage. Stern-faced in their beards and turbans, they seemed to be wearing more jewellery than you could hope to find in a Bond Street jeweller's window. The rest were wearing frock coats like any civilised gentleman, though a couple had a taste for what looked like disreputably loud silk waistcoats.

He turned the next page and halted. He stared at the photograph for a long moment. Then he read the caption beneath.

The Maharajah of Ishri Bihar, with his daughter Princess Alexandrina

'Who's that you're looking at then?' Mildred had come back downstairs, She peered over his shoulder.

Caught unawares, David tapped the photograph. 'I couldn't swear to it, but I think I've seen her.'

'Down by the docks?' Mildred said with disbelief. 'When?'

'Just in passing, a few days ago, maybe,' David said uncomfortably. He wished he'd kept his mouth shut.

Mrs Jessop leaned over to see who they were talking about. 'Princess Alexandrina? Oh, I shouldn't wonder if it was her. She's patroness of a charity for distressed seamen or such. Very active by all accounts, likes to see exactly where the money's going. Lives in Richmond. Her father sent her to England to be educated, which is why she goes by a decent Christian name. That and her godfather's the Prince of Wales. Her uncle is one of his set. Hunts foxes with his Royal Highness in Leicestershire and tigers back home. That's what the papers say, anyway.'

She spoke with such certainty that David didn't doubt her. He knew women were good with such things. His mum could relate every detail of his cousins' lives, even the ones he would struggle to pick out of a crowd.

'Well I never.' Mildred lost interest. She made a final adjustment to her straw bonnet with its bright paper flowers, as blue as her sparkling eyes. 'Where we going then, Davey?'

He dragged his thoughts back to the matter in hand. 'I thought we'd take a turn around the park and then go for some tea?'

'That sounds nice.' Mildred smiled happily.

David didn't think she was quite so pleased with him by the time he escorted her back down the area steps to the tradesman's door. Hand on heart, he had done his best to put the mysterious lady out of his mind, but his thoughts kept drifting back to that curious encounter. Mildred had been forced to repeat something she'd just said at least half a dozen times over the course of their afternoon.

As he headed back to his lodgings at considerably faster than regulation pace, he decided two things. Firstly, he'd take Mildred to see Buffalo Bill Cody's Wild West Circus at the American Exhibition in Earl's Court. That should make things up between them. Secondly, one way or another, he would find out if he really had met this unconventional princess.

Mildred's next half day didn't coincide with his own next day off. David tried not to feel too relieved about that as he took the first of the succession of omnibuses that would carry him all the way out to Richmond. The journey took most of the morning, and he was forced to turn a blind eye to unscheduled stops to pick up additional passengers, or when there were far too many folk crammed aboard for the labouring, sweating horses. He wasn't in uniform, so it wasn't as if he could take any official notice of such offences.

When he finally disembarked on Richmond High Street, he looked around for a tobacconist. In his experience, they knew what was what in their neck of the woods. Once he was inside the shop, he studied the selection of pipes on offer while he waited for an elderly man to make his choice of smokes, and for a liveried footman to collect some cigars.

'Can I help you, officer?' the grey-haired man behind the counter asked, as the shop door closed behind the footman.

David turned around. On the one hand it was a bit humiliating to be so easily recognised as a policeman. On the other hand, it saved him having to persuade the man he had good reason to be asking questions. It wasn't as if he carried any official identification. His truncheon had his division letter and warrant number painted on it, but he could hardly have brought that on all those omnibuses.

'What gave me away?'

The tobacconist nodded at his feet. 'Your boots.'

'Right.' David made a mental note to remember that when he joined the detective branch. 'Can you give me directions to the Indian princess's house? Princess Alexandrina,' he added.

The man looked at him with a measuring eye. 'How many princesses do you think we've got around here?'

Then he came to some conclusion and briskly explained the route David needed to take. David thanked him and made a quick stop at a nearby cafe for a much needed mug of tea and a currant bun. Then he made his way to a shady corner on the tree-lined street where the princess lived. It was soon apparent that the tobacconist had dealt fairly with him. At least half of the servants David saw going in and out were dark-complexioned.

What now? David leaned against the tree and wondered how long he might have to wait before he got a glimpse of the lady herself. How long could he afford to wait, if he was going to get back to his lodgings at a reasonable hour? Too late, and Mrs Shaw would want to know where he'd been. Was there any way he could knock on the door and —

Lost in thought, his knees buckled when a heavy hand landed on his shoulder. As David recovered his balance, that firm grip turned him around. David found himself face to face with a tall, broad-shouldered African wearing a suit just like any English gentleman. David realised his captor had come up behind him on silent feet, shielded by the tree.

'Good afternoon, Constable Price.' There was a hint of amusement in the big man's resonant voice. He had an unfamiliar accent, but there could be no doubt that his English was perfectly fluent.

David swallowed hard but his throat was as dry as dust. 'Good – good –'

'Her highness sends her compliments,' the man said smoothly, 'and invites you to join her for some tea.'

'I – thank you,' David said hoarsely.

He thought fast. He couldn't turn down this opportunity, could he? That and he didn't want to think what the consequences might be if he declined. There could be no doubting the lady's rank and influence now.

The African gentleman removed his hand from David's shoulder. He led the way across the road and through the garden gate. As they made their way up the gleaming white steps towards the front entrance of the house, David suddenly wondered if he had miscalculated. If the African tried to drag him off the street, there was a good chance some passer-by might intervene. Once he was behind that heavy wooden door though, anything might happen. It wasn't as if anyone knew he was here. He clenched his fists. He realised his hands were clammy with sweat, and not just from the hot day.

A uniformed maid with a bronzed complexion and exotic features opened the door to the big man's knock. He walked into the house without looking to see that David was following. The maid waited by the open door, smiling. She wouldn't be able to stop him if he turned tail and ran. Of course, if he did that, he would never find out what this was all about.

David drew a deep breath and stepped across the threshold. There wasn't a speck of dirt on the hallway's patterned tiles, and the mahogany hallstand gleamed with polish. The African gentleman was entering a room at the far end, still without a backward glance. The intervening doors were closed.

'May I take your hat, sir?' the maid prompted. Whatever her parentage, her accent was pure Whitechapel.

'Yes, of course.' David snatched off his bowler and handed it over.

'Her highness is expecting you.' The maid nodded meaningfully towards the door at the end of the hall, still ajar.

'Right. Thank you.' David squared his shoulders and advanced, trying desperately to quell his nerves.

The open door led him into a charming drawing room which overlooked a rose garden. The fragrance of the summer's blooms drifted in through the open windows, together with flourishes of birdsong. An elegant sofa and a scatter of chairs upholstered in gold brocade surrounded a low, rosewood table. Sitting on the sofa and leaning forward, an Indian lady in a sky-blue afternoon gown was pouring tea from a silver pot into a fine bone china cup. She handed that to the African gentleman who was now seated at his ease on the chair to her right. As she topped up the pot with hot water from the matching silver jug, she looked up at David.

'Would you like a cup of tea, Constable Price? I always find it wonderfully cooling, even in this beastly hot weather. Please, take a seat. Do you take milk and sugar?' Her hand moved towards the milk jug and the sugar tongs.

David's lurid, incoherent fears evaporated, leaving him feeling very foolish. Foolish and more puzzled than ever. Now he had heard her speak, it was clear she was the mysterious woman he had met. Equally obviously, now he saw her sitting in this airy room, she was indeed the maharajah's daughter whose photograph he had seen in the newspaper.

'Yes, please, two lumps, thank you.' He sat down on the chair opposite Princess Alexandrina. 'Thank you, your highness – my lady – ma'am.'

She leaned forward to hand David his cup. 'Did Abidugun introduce himself?'

'I – no – that's to say...' David glanced at the stern-faced African.

The dark-complexioned man's expression didn't change. 'Abidugun Sangodele, at your service.'

'Constable David Price, at yours.' He fervently hoped he wouldn't be called on to repeat that jaw-cracker. He had no idea how to spell such an outlandish name, come to that.

The princess's smile was amused. 'Have you come to retrieve your handkerchief? I'm afraid it was beyond salvaging. I will of course replace it.'

'What? No – that is to say...' David took the tea and drank it hastily before he could spill it. As it was, the rattle of the cup in the saucer sounded as loud as gunfire to him in this quiet room. As he set it down on the table, he stole a sideways glance at the African. Mr Sangodele was sipping his tea, looking back at David with a faint, mocking smile of his own.

Before the young constable could feel affronted, the princess spoke again. 'Would you be so kind as to satisfy my curiosity, Constable Price? Why did you intervene, when you saw our associate being attacked on the docks, on the night we first met?'

The briefest sweep of her sapphire-ringed hand included the African in her question. David had already guessed he must have been one of the shadowy figures who had escorted her.

'Not every policeman would risk his own skin to save a black man from a beating,' Mr Sangodele said bluntly.

'What others might do is between them and their conscience. I do my sworn duty to keep the peace.' David cleared his throat. 'May I ask, how did you know I was outside your house today?'

'Mr Gluckstein sent his boy with a note, after you had made enquiries in his shop.' The princess looked steadily across the tea table. 'Not everyone who comes to my door does so with good intentions. So I must ask, what is your business with me?'

David decided to go for broke. He'd come clear across London to get here, and he still had to get back to his lodgings before dark. 'There was something odd going on that night, and I think you should know about it, ma'am, since you're a patroness of that Asiatic sailors' refuge.'

She arched a fine dark eyebrow. 'You are quite the detective, aren't you? Please, do go on.'

'We got called off our beats because we were told those Lascars were fighting down at the hostel. Only, when we arrived, there was no trouble to be seen. That report could have been an honest mistake, of course, or some bit of bother could have fizzled out, but that doesn't explain why there were so many Africans outside the place, nor yet why a whole troop of Chinese turned up.'

He couldn't help glancing at the African gentleman. The man looked enigmatically at him. David drew a resolute breath and continued.

'As long as there was no trouble, I wouldn't have thought much more about it. But a gang of riff-raff from the docks arrived and they were spoiling for a fight. They'd have got one too, if they hadn't seen they were outnumbered. So I have to ask myself, how did those other – other *foreigners* know the Lascars were going to be attacked? Come to that, who told my sergeant, and why?' For the moment, David decided, he'd keep his uneasy suspicions about Sergeant Shaw and those looks from the leaders of the mob to himself.

The princess folded dainty hands in her lap. 'What do you know about Lascars, Constable?'

That was unexpected, but he could see he would have to answer her if he were to get anything in return. 'They're sailors from India's western shores who hire on with ships sailing for English ports. When they arrive, some of them go looking for opportunities ashore. That doesn't always work out as well as they hoped.'

The princess smiled, this time entirely without humour. 'I regret to tell you the reality is very different. By and large, these are men who have been thrown off their farms as the British Empire extends its reach over India. They go to sea as a last, desperate resort. The ship owners are very well aware of this, and consequently believe they can mistreat them with impunity. At best, these men are brutalised and fed wholly inadequate rations. At worst?' She shook her head for a moment.

'Some captains find it amusing to offer Hindus the choice of eating beef or starving, once they are out of sight of land. These captains know full well such meat is forbidden to those of the Hindu faith. Others will offer pork to Muslims in similar fashion. Lascars are frequently and savagely beaten for the slightest offence, real or imagined. Some die from their injuries and their corpses are tossed overboard without the rites of any religion. Do you wonder that those who have seen such atrocities flee those ships as soon as they can?'

She didn't wait for David to reply. He could hear the anger in her tone. 'Others are crippled by shipboard accidents or mistreatment. Those unfortunates are dumped on England's docks as soon as the vessel ties up, left destitute. Once the cargo has been unloaded, the rest are frequently denied even the meagre wages they were promised. They are told their only hope of seeing their homes again is to sign on for the return voyage and to work for free. If that particular vessel isn't sailing back to India, they are simply thrown off the ship to find whatever work they can ashore, forced to beg, or to starve. The ship owners wash their hands of all responsibility, leaving them prey to those who make their lives more wretched still with the false solace of alcohol or opium. This is the reality of life for the unfortunates subjugated by your glorious British Empire, Constable. Do you honestly believe such wretched men would fight each other for no reason?'

David had broken up pub fights that started because someone disliked the colour of someone else's boots. He decided not to say so, when he realised that some response was expected from him.

'What's any of that got to do with a clockwork rat?' The words were out before he could stop himself.

The princess stiffened, and the African gentleman leaned forward in his chair, as though he was about to stand up. David tried not to show just how much that unnerved him. The princess sprang to her feet. That startled him even more.

She looked down at David with a challenging glint in her eye. 'Let me show you.'

'Highness?' Mr Sangodele rose from his chair. His tone was somewhere between surprise and a warning.

The princess glanced at him. 'Who is he going to tell? Who would believe him, if he did? Who in Whitehall or Scotland Yard would sanction searching this house, when they know I can end their career with a telegram?'

The African gentleman had no answer to that. The princess turned her dazzling smile on David. 'Please come with me.'

She left the room, and David followed. He was very well aware of Mr Sangodele following them. Now though, he was too intrigued to feel that uneasy. He followed the princess to a door halfway along the hall. She threw open the door to what David would ordinarily expect to be some private sitting room, or perhaps a library in a house of this size.

The walls were certainly lined with shelves, but rather than being filled with books these were stacked with boxes of varying size. Some were made of metal, and others of brass-bound wood. Gaps here and there held trays of tools. Over by the window, where the light was best, four men and two ladies sat around a table covered with a green baize cloth. All were wearing jewellers' eye-glasses, intent on assembling a variety of mechanisms from tiny cogwheels and such. At first glance, none looked to be of British parentage, though they were perfectly respectably dressed. After meeting the maid who had answered the door, David wasn't prepared to hazard a guess as to their origins. He was also pretty sure they weren't making clocks or pocket watches.

The second baize-covered table in the middle of the Turkish-carpeted room was even more bemusing. A Chinese gentleman and two young ladies who might or might not be related to him were busily scrutinising minute slips of ivory or bone with the aid of large magnifying lenses. Every so often they would slip a handful of the tiny white rectangles into the different sections of a wooden tray clearly purpose-built to hold them. Occasionally, one was rejected, tossed aside into a brass bowl.

The greatest puzzle was on the far side of the room. A young Indian man and an English woman of mature years sat at a small table taking cards from a box and sorting them into neat stacks. These were neither playing cards nor visiting cards, but were plain white and punched with numerous holes. Behind them stood an astonishingly complex – *device*? David couldn't think of any adequate word to describe the contrivance. It appeared to be principally made from numerous, interlaced columns of toothed brass cogwheels inscribed with numbers. There were also what looked like drive belts as well as axles and levers, together with handles to crank various parts of the machine. All told, there were intricacies and complexities that he couldn't hope to fathom. He had never seen anything like it.

He realised that the English lady sorting the cards was looking at him. Her lips curved with a slight smile when she caught his eye. She nodded reassuringly and returned to her task. Several of the others around the room glanced briefly at him, and continued their work unperturbed.

David turned to the princess whose face was alight with amusement. 'You don't need to worry about me telling anyone what I've seen in this room, ma'am. I wouldn't know where to start. I have no idea what's going on.'

The princess walked to a shelf and took down a box. She opened it to show David a mechanical rat. If it wasn't the one he had found by the river, now repaired, it was an identical toy.

'You were wondering how so many of Mr Sangodele's compatriots knew there was going to be trouble at the Lascar Hostel? How Mr Lam here knew to alert his countrymen?' The princess walked towards the middle table where the Chinese trio continued their work without looking up. She picked a discarded slip out of the brass bowl and handed it to David. 'We use these little creatures to carry messages. They can be instructed where to go by means of these miniature cards stacked in the right sequence.'

Now David could examine it closely, he saw the tiny piece of ivory was pierced with pinpricks. There was also a miniscule crack which presumably explained why it had been discarded. He tossed it back in the bowl and looked across to the card-sorting table.

'Very good,' the princess approved. 'The principle is the same. Though Mrs Bradshaw and Mr Bhaskar use those cards to instruct the analytical engine to devise the best routes for our rats to follow, amongst various other things.'

David gazed at the vast brass contrivance and wondered how much it weighed. 'That's what that is, I take it?'

'It is,' the princess said proudly. 'The great and good of London's scientific establishment said it could never be built, and, granted, the original design was for an absolute colossus. It never occurred to them to try a different approach. We on the other hand, have created a far less cumbersome device, as we do not assume as an article of faith that a British gentleman's scientific design cannot be improved. Since we are willing to learn from each other, this analytical engine combines the expertise with working bronze honed over generations by Mr Sangodele's ancestors with my own compatriots' skills in creating automata, and our Chinese friends' excellence at carving intricate miniatures in ivory and other materials.'

'I can only assume these scientific gentlemen never visit the British Museum,' the African gentleman said dourly. 'Examples of such fine craftsmanship have been plundered from every corner of the Empire. But there are none so blind as those who refuse to see.'

'Well I never.' David could see that some response was called for, even if he was still struggling to make sense of what he was hearing. Mechanical rats carrying messages across London? Who would ever believe that? He frowned. Where did the warnings the rats carried come from?

'But how did you know the hostel was going to be attacked in the first place?'

The princess and Mr Sangodele exchanged a glance that David couldn't read. She held the tall, dark man's gaze and raised her eyebrows. David realised that everyone else in the room was discreetly watching for his answer. After a long moment, Mr Sangodele answered her unspoken question with an infinitesimal nod. The tension around the green baize tables didn't abate, though. If anything, the air of expectation grew more intense.

'Please, come this way.' The princess smiled with satisfaction as she turned and left the room.

David did as he was told. Once again, he was conscious of Mr Sangodele following close behind him with noiseless steps.

The princess opened the next door along the hallway. This had once been some gentleman's study. Now a bony youth with a shock of red hair and a suit of clothes even cheaper than David's sat at a small table reading a weighty book. At least the constable recognised the apparatus the boy was attending. It was a needle telegraph, of the sort that used Bright's bells. Paper and pencils were ready for the lad to record any communications he received, and to encode those he was asked to send.

The youth sprang to his feet. 'Did you want to send a message, madam?' His accent was unmistakably Irish.

'Not at the moment, Francis, thank you. We are just showing our guest around.' The princess closed the door again.

As they returned to the rose-scented drawing room, David wondered if having your own private telegraph system was entirely legal. He rather thought the Post Office would have something to say about that. He decided that was a question for someone far above his own rank.

The tea things had been cleared away. The princess resumed her seat on the sofa and David took the same chair as before. Mr Sangodele walked across the room to gaze out at the garden through an open window.

The constable looked across the exquisite table. 'Where are the telegraph wires?'

It hadn't occurred to him to look for any such thing while he was waiting outside, but he was certain he would have noticed something so far out of the ordinary on this quiet, prosperous street.

The princess grinned like a child delighting in some mischief. 'We have created all manner of automata and some are far smaller than the rats. We used the very smallest to pull telegraph cables through the gas pipes that serve the street lights. Isn't that ingenious?'

'Truly astonishing, ma'am,' David said honestly.

Mr Sangodele turned away from the window, though he did not come back to sit down. 'I must ask for your word, Constable Price, that you will tell no one of the mechanicals and other contraptions you have seen in this house. I swear to you that we only use them for honest purposes. If they were to be discovered and copied, though, there's no knowing what nefarious purposes these things might be put to.'

'I regret we cannot trust the Imperial powers not to use such discoveries to further oppress us, instead of to our mutual benefit.' The princess seemed genuinely regretful about that.

'I can imagine.' David had already been thinking how criminals could use such devices. 'I'll give you my oath, and gladly. This house's secrets are safe with me.'

'Thank you. Now, let me answer your earlier question,' Mr Sangodele went on briskly. 'Young Francis is not the only Irishman in our ranks, though if you were to meet any of his brethren along the riverside, you would swear they had been born in Poplar. They make a point of associating with the rowdier elements, so they can warn us when mischief is brewing. That night you and I met, they heard that trouble was being deliberately stirred up by strangers visiting the dockside pubs. These men had plenty of money to buy beer and gin to fuel a riot. This is by no means the first time they have stirred up hatred against some easily singled-out group, and this is happening more and more often of late. We keep a close watch on likely trouble spots, but sooner or later, we won't be alerted in time.'

The princess looked straight at David. 'We did not expect to see the police there. We certainly did not expect to see them before any alarm could have been raised. We would very much like to know who had advance knowledge that trouble was likely. Will you help us find out? That may well lead us to whoever is behind this malice. Once we know that, we can hope to learn why.'

David wanted an answer to those questions himself, but first and foremost he still had a duty to keep the queen's peace. If there were Irishmen involved – well, it wasn't so very long since hooligans agitating for an independent Irish state had plagued London and other cities with their dynamite campaigns.

He looked the princess in the eye and squared his shoulders. 'That depends what you will do with that knowledge, your highness. I won't be party to any outrages, not by way of retaliation nor anything else.'

'I am very glad to hear it,' she assured him. 'Do you know the Golden Rule, Constable?'

'And as ye would that men should do to you, do ye also to them likewise,' David said automatically. 'Luke, chapter six, verse thirty-one.' Mrs Williams made sure that every child who attended chapel knew that particular scripture.

'Quite so, and that commandment is also to be found in St Mark's Gospel, chapter seven, verse twelve.' The princess looked at him intently. 'Would it surprise you to learn that the same precept can be found in the ancient Sanskrit text of the Mahabharata? In the writings of Confucius, whose philosophies Mr Lam and his countrymen espouse? In the writings of the prophet Mohammed, whom our Muslim friends revere? Abidugun can tell you how such wisdom is expressed by the Yoruba people.' She gestured towards Mr Sangodele.

'We all abide by this principle, I can promise you, Constable. You saw for yourself that no one on our side raised a hand outside the hostel. Once we know who is behind this and what their motives might be, we will find peaceful ways to dissuade them. As you can see, I have ample resources.' A wave of her hand indicated their opulent surroundings. 'My family finds it very profitable, as well as wholly prudent, not to challenge the Empire. I am supposed to occupy myself and my purse with good works as befits a lady. So that is what I am doing.'

David wondered what the princess's family would make of her unusual interpretation of charitable endeavours.

Mr Sangodele came to sit down. He was glowering once again, though not at anyone in particular. 'All our different homelands have learned the bloody folly of attacking the British. Not just the British. The leaders of Europe's great powers have been sitting in smoke-filled rooms in Berlin, these past few years. They carve up the world like a roast fowl, with every glutton demanding his share.'

He shook his head. 'We have no wish to bring down the Empire's fury on our countrymen's heads. We know that violence here will be seized on, and used as an excuse to extend and strengthen the army's hold abroad. All the while, of course, they will claim to be protecting our interests.'

'We choose to play the long game,' the princess said serenely. 'No empire lasts forever. Our own histories tell us that, going back to the centuries before William of Normandy ever set foot on these shores. The great Chinese dynasties have come and gone. The Mughals rose and fell. Even once-mighty Ottoman power is now in decline. So we work together to protect our own people while we bide our time. After all, the Empire has given a shared language and brought us together here in London where we can share our skills and knowledge. When Britannia no longer rules the waves, we will step forward.' Her confidence was unshakeable.

'So will you help us?' she asked David a moment later, 'to frustrate those out to cause trouble that we want no part of? To uncover what lies behind this malice?'

'Or is this none of your concern?' Mr Sangodele challenged him.

David's hackles rose. 'Have you ever heard of a Welsh stick, your highness?'

His glance took in Mr Sangodele as well as the princess. To his satisfaction, he saw they were equally nonplussed. David explained.

'Both classes in my school back home had one, infants and juniors. You were given it to hold if you were caught speaking Welsh instead of English. It could only be passed on to the next child found guilty of the same offence.'

He could hear his words softening into the lyrical accent he had grown up with. The accent he had learned to conceal, so no one here in London would guess that David Price would once have been called Dafydd ap Rhys.

'At the end of the day, whichever child was still holding the stick was rapped across the knuckles with it, punished hard, for the sin of using the language they learned at their mother's knee.

You don't have to come from over the sea to know the heavy hand of the English.'

He realised Mr Sangodele and the princess were looking at him with fixed expressions. He recalled some of the tales of English reprisals after the Indian Mutiny, and various newspaper reports of more recent military action in Southern Africa.

'It's not the same, of course,' David said hastily, 'but still.'

There was another long moment of silence, broken only by birdsong in the garden.

'But still,' the princess agreed. 'So, will you help us?'

'I will.' David nodded. 'There was definitely something not right about that night.'

He told them then about the meaningful looks he'd seen pass between the sergeant and the leaders of the mob. 'And Sergeant Shaw was ready to believe the very worst of the Lascars. He'd have us believe the foulest rumours too, even though I can't recall any official record of half the things he claimed.'

The princess's smooth brow creased in thought. 'So who is telling him such things? How might we find out?'

Mr Sangodele looked at David with a challenge in his dark eyes. 'Do you suppose he might tell a trusted ally?'

'I think he might well,' David said cautiously, 'but how do we convince him I'm to be trusted?'

THREE

Don't ask a question, if you don't think you'll like the answer. David couldn't recall where he'd heard that particular piece of wisdom, but he wished he had remembered it in that drawing room in Richmond. Though, to be honest, he couldn't think of an alternative to Mr Sangodele's plan. Heaven only knows, he had tried.

He concentrated on maintaining his regulation pace. Walk too quickly, and he might arrive too soon. Walk too slowly and he risked losing sight of Sergeant Shaw. His superior was walking a hundred feet or so ahead as they both headed back to the tenement. Hopefully he was unaware of the constable dogging his footsteps.

It had been a long and thankfully uneventful night shift. Even the drunks seemed to find the weather too hot for fighting. That was all about to change. David braced himself as he heard running feet in a nearby alley. He continued walking steadily. There must be no suspicion that he had any idea what was going to happen next.

Three masked men with skin as dark as their ragged clothes burst out of the alley. David saw that much before one of them punched him in the face. Then all he saw was stars. He staggered into the pool of light cast by a street lamp and collapsed, as had been agreed. His attackers started to kick him, not nearly as viciously as they could have done, but hard enough to leave convincing bruises. As he doubled up to protect his balls from accidents, David very rapidly regretted agreeing to that.

'Sarge! Sarge! Help!' He shouted as loudly as he could, but he made no attempt to use his whistle. There was only one person they wanted coming to David's rescue. To his relief, he heard heavy boots rushing towards him, loud on the pavement.

'Oy oy oy! What the fuck do you think you're doing, you black bastards?'

David winced as another hard kick hit his thigh. Thankfully that was the last, although his assailants mimed a few more assaults. David knew they had to make sure Sergeant Shaw got a good look at them before they fled.

The sergeant's boots arrived. The attackers fled. Using the street lamp for support, David struggled to his feet, acting as though he was far more severely hurt. As Shaw reached him, David saw the sergeant was about to blow his whistle. He lurched towards him, knocking the whistle from his hand as if by accident.

'Oh, Sarge,' he gasped, clinging to the man to make it impossible for him to give chase. 'Thank God you was there. Did you get a good look at them? Did you see where they went?' That was a genuine question. That first punch had split the skin just above David's eyebrow, and blood obscured his view.

'Scarves around their faces, the filthy devils. God alone knows where they've gone.' The sergeant turned his attention to David and slipped an arm around his waist. 'Can you walk, lad?'

'Yes. Ow!' David yelped as the sergeant's arm found what would undoubtedly be a convincing bruise. He gritted his teeth. 'If you could just help me...'

As they staggered along together, David breathed a little easier. It was all very well the princess telling him not to worry if Mr Sangodele's men were caught, but it was undeniably true this first phase of their plan would go more smoothly if they escaped.

It wasn't far to the tenement. That was another good thing, David soon decided. Walking in this awkward crouch, pretending he had been more seriously injured, was making his back ache far more than any of the thumps he had taken.

As the sergeant opened the grimy building's ground floor door, David took the opportunity to disentangle himself from Shaw's supporting arm. He clung to the bannister and began to climb the stairs one at a time. 'I'll be all right, Sarge.'

'You take it slow and careful.' Shaw skirted past him to take the steps two at a time. Up above, he threw open the tenement door. 'Betsy! Betsy!'

As David reached the top of the stairs, Mrs Shaw appeared wrapping her dressing gown over her nightdress. She started asking questions, ten to the dozen as she knotted the belt. Shaw wasn't listening, more concerned with condemning David's assailants in the vilest terms. With both of them talking over each other, it was impossible to hear what either one was saying. David gave up the attempt, letting Mrs Shaw lead him into the kitchen. His stomach rumbled as he caught the scent of sausages waiting for them on the back of the hotplate.

'You sit down, and let's clean you up.' Mrs Shaw pressed him down into a chair and pulled her apron off its peg.

She bustled away to fetch clean rags and filled a shallow bowl with hot water from the kettle sitting on the range. David didn't have to pretend to wince when she wiped the blood out of his eyes and from his forehead. That cut above his eyebrow really stung.

'You'll need court-plaster on that, else it'll leave a mark.' She tutted as she cut a square from the next sheet in the book of patent wound dressings. 'Keep still. Now, 'old that tight while it sticks.'

David let her position his hand to keep the isinglass-coated silk in place, once she had used it to draw the edges of the cut together. He pressed hard. Mildred wouldn't be impressed if he ended up with an unsightly scar.

The sergeant had finally exhausted his store of invective about filthy 'eathens and foreigners. As his wife busied herself fetching their dinners, he sat on the chair opposite, and studied David's face.

'Looks worse than it is, lad,' he said, bracing. 'Mind you, you'll have two lovely black eyes.'

David managed a dutiful grin as Shaw trilled those last four words to the tune of the musical hall comic song.

'What's going on, Sarge? There's not this sort of trouble as a rule. Then there was that other night, down by the Lascar Hostel. Something's just not right. What are we going to do?'

For a dreadful moment, he thought he had gone too far. Across the table, Shaw had stiffened. Now his gaze was searching David's face. The young constable tried to look as woebegone as possible. Then Mrs Shaw put their plates down on the table.

'Eat up and you'll feel better. I'll make a nice pot of tea.' She fetched cutlery for them both, and busied herself with the kettle once again.

Satisfied that the plaster was now solidly stuck, David applied himself to his meal. He was ravenously hungry. He did sneak a few looks across the table at Shaw. The sergeant didn't notice. He seemed lost in thought as he ate his sausages and mash. David cast around for something else he might say, to convince the man they were on the same side in this mysterious strife. On the other hand, he didn't want to arouse suspicion. Inspiration failed him. Then he recalled the princess's words. Perhaps this was a time for him to play the long game too.

'This hour, it's 'ardly worth my while going back to bed.' Mrs Shaw set down full mugs of tea and bustled off, presumably to get dressed.

David finished eating and drank his tea. He stood up with a grimace. That beating might not have been in earnest, but he was still stiffening up. 'Sleep well, Sarge.'

'What?' Shaw had been miles away. 'Yes, you too, lad.'

David made his way to his room. The curtains were drawn and he was able to undress and get to bed in the gloom before the others started stirring. When Ralph in the bed by the window let in the daylight, and the three of them started bickering over whose turn it was to fetch shaving water for the washstand, David pulled a fold of blanket over his head. Spared questions about what had happened to his face, he soon fell deeply asleep despite his bruises. He had barely got any rest the night before, anxious about what was going to happen.

The smell of bacon woke him up some while later. He opened his eyes to see Shaw standing by his bed. The sergeant had a mug of tea in one hand and held a plate in the other. He waited while David sat up. Handing over the food and drink, he sat down on the closest bed. 'Eat up.'

'Thanks, Sarge.' David discovered fried onions along with the bacon sandwiched between the thick slabs of bread. As he ate, he noticed Shaw was staring at the floor, pondering something as deeply as he had done over their dinner. David also realised it was far earlier in the afternoon than he was used to waking up, and Shaw was in his Sunday suit, not the uniform he wore on duty and off. Something was afoot.

He put the empty mug on the crumb-strewn plate and set them both down on the floor. 'You were right, Sarge. Last night, that trouble wasn't nearly as bad as it could have been. Thank the good Lord you were close by. I definitely owe you one.'

Shaw looked up. 'What do you think about messages from the other side, Price? Existence beyond the veil? Spirits guiding us and all that?'

'Well, I –' Taken completely by surprise, David answered honestly. 'I don't know what to make of the notion, truth be told. My mum would call it ungodly, but science tells us there's all manner of things we can't see, like electricity and magnetism. There's Doctor Lister and his talk of germs, and the queen herself believes in him. They say there's different gases in the air we breathe, and that one creature can turn into another, even if that takes thousands of years.' He thought back to the upper room in Richmond and the unexpected marvels there. 'Who's to say what they'll discover next?'

'That's right.' Shaw looked at him for another long moment.

David recalled someone at the station saying something about the Shaws having a son who had been a soldier. A soldier who died in the attempt to reach Khartoum and rescue General Gordon. He had been the couple's only child, so Albert had said. That's why Mrs Shaw was so motherly towards the young constables. Had the sergeant turned to spiritualism to ease his grief?

'Well rested, are you?' Shaw asked him briskly. 'Want to come along with me and see something interesting? We'll be back before it's time for parade.'

David nodded as casually as he could. 'All right.'

Shaw stood up. 'Quick as you can, lad. We don't want to be late.'

David threw back the blankets as the sergeant left the room. As usual there was only a splash of cold water left in the washstand jug, but he was used to shaving with that. He saw bruises and scrapes he hadn't been aware of reflected in the washstand mirror. It was a safe bet that Mildred wouldn't be walking out with him again until he looked less like a man who'd lost a prize fight. When they went to the park, she expected to be the one who was drawing admiring eyes. On the credit side of the ledger, that court-plaster was still closing the cut on his forehead which seemed to be healing cleanly.

He dressed, and found the sergeant waiting for him in the kitchen. They went downstairs and out of the soot-stained building's front door. David eased the rim of his bowler hat a little lower down, careful of his cut but wanting to shield his blackened eyes from curious stares.

Thankfully, their destination wasn't far away. Sergeant Shaw led him to a street where what must once have been grand merchant's houses were now let as individual rooms. Shaw walked up to a front door whose fresh coat of paint was in sharp contrast to the rest of the shabby street. He knocked confidently.

The door was opened by a middle-aged woman in a long black dress. 'We thought you wasn't coming.'

'Sorry about that.' Shaw snatched off his hat and turned to David. 'I brought this lad along. I hope that's all right. He got caught up in some bother last night, and I reckon he could use some guidance. Constable Price, this is Madam Saint Cloud.'

'All seekers after truth are welcome here.' She smiled and stepped back to allow them to enter.

Shaw headed for the front room of the house. As David followed, clutching his own hat, he didn't know what to think. He had never seen the sarge act so humble. More than that, it was clear to a blind man that Shaw was the one who had come here looking for answers.

As for the lady, well, David would wager sixpence to a gold watch that 'Saint Cloud' wasn't the name she'd been born with, nor yet married into since she wore no wedding ring. He was doing his best not to stare. She had ropes of jet beads hung around her neck and her wrists were heavy with silver bracelets. Most striking of all, her unbound white hair reached right down to her waist.

She followed them into the front room, where half a dozen people were already sitting at a large round table covered with a fringed purple velvet cloth. The walls were hung with an array of peculiar pictures, ranging from a tumbledown tower to a seated woman in a crown holding up a sword and a set of scales.

'Get another chair, Gerald,' the white-haired woman said briskly.

A thin-faced young man in a brown suit and with ink stains on his shirt cuffs got up to fetch an upright chair from a row set against the far wall. Evidently the table could accommodate far larger gatherings than this afternoon's assembly.

David swiftly assessed those present as everyone shuffled to one side or the other to make space for the new arrival. Two of the women looked like mother and daughter, well-dressed and in trade rather than service, he guessed. The other two were almost certainly maids, though without their uniforms he had no idea if their duties would be up in the nursery, down in the scullery or anywhere in between. The last man, burly and bewhiskered, who sat beside the empty chair that the sergeant was taking, looked to be a butcher or baker or something of that sort. David decided to think of him as a butcher until proven otherwise.

He hesitated before taking his own seat. 'Is there anything I can do to help? Draw the curtains perhaps?' Swags of more purple velvet hung from beaded pelmets in the deep bay window.

The white-haired woman was busy with a box on a sideboard. She looked round. 'Oh no, dear, there's no need for that. It's charlatans and frauds who hide their tricks with shadows and candlelight. We use a psychic telegraph for our séances, clear as day for all to see. Sit yourself down.'

Red-faced, David did as he was told. The rest of the company were already sitting with joined hands and most of them had closed their eyes, the sergeant included. David watched as the white-haired woman set some sort of apparatus on the table, at arm's length in front of her chair. She could see that he was looking, as she set the whatever-it-was down with its face towards him. She met his gaze and smiled, then went to fetch a pencil and a sheaf of paper from the sideboard.

David studied the device. It resembled a mantelpiece clock, though it clearly wasn't one. For a start, it only had a single hand. There was no glass protecting the dial, and no wooden case behind it, where a clock's movement might have been housed. The white circle was mounted on a single inch-thick piece of mahogany. That sat on a flat base with four little feet to raise it above the tablecloth.

The letters of the alphabet were enamelled around the outer edge of the dial, and he could see words radiating out from the centre like the spokes of a wheel. These separated the numerals, one to ten, inscribed in a smaller circle inside the alphabet. David did his best to read the words. He'd got as far as 'Yes', 'Doubtful', 'No', 'Don't Know', 'I Think So', and 'A Mistake', when the white-haired woman clapped briskly and sat down directly opposite him.

'Let us open our minds to the great beyond, to seek the wisdom of those who see all now that they have been freed from the physical bonds of this mortal plane.' She reached out to clasp hands with the shop-girl to her right and with Gerald to her left.

She locked eyes with David, and now her expression was challenging him. To his right, the elder of the two maids groped for the hand she was clearly expecting to find. To his left, the butcher simply snapped his fingers before turning his palm upwards. Reluctantly, David reached out to join the circle and closed his eyes.

Silence filled the room. He could hear everyone else's steady breathing. The maid's moist hand trembled under his own, and David had to fight the urge to give her fingers a reassuring squeeze. The butcher's grip was cool and steady. For a long moment, nothing seemed to be happening. Then a swift whirring noise made him open his eyes. The single hand in the centre of the dial was spinning around, counter-clockwise.

He was relieved to see that everyone else was looking at the thing too. The maid and the butcher released their hold on him. Around the table, the others were doing the same. Everyone watched the dial intently. The hand stopped and David saw the device was designed so that the metal arm would underline one of the spoke-like words.

Sergeant Shaw read it aloud. 'A message.'

A frisson of anticipation ran around the table. David felt a shiver run down his own spine.

'A – D – E – L –' The sergeant read the letters aloud as the hand moved on.

The white-haired woman looked up from writing on her paper. 'Adelaide?'

The hand on the dial spun around to underline the word 'Yes'.

Shaw relayed this, since Madam Saint Cloud couldn't see what the telegraph's face might be indicating.

'Ooh,' the maid to David's right whispered to him. 'She was killed in the Indian Mutiny. Dreadful business.' Her eyes gleamed avidly.

The hand moved again to spell out more words. Those with a less clear view shuffled their chairs around the table to see the dial more clearly. Only the white-haired woman stayed where she was, with the back of the device towards her. She concentrated on her writing; first the individual letters and then the whole words when the psychic telegraph agreed with someone's suggestion around the table. The maid to David's right offered non-stop guesses from the very first letter.

Everyone here was clearly used to this way of taking down the messages, but David found it impossible to follow what the telegraph was saying, with so many voices talking over each other. He concentrated instead on trying to work out how the trick was done.

For the life of him, he couldn't see what was moving the busy hand. There were no wires leading to the device and there had been no sign of anything under the tablecloth when the white-haired woman had put it down. The fringe of the cloth barely brushed his knees, and while he couldn't look under the table without arousing suspicion, David was ready to swear there was nothing and nobody hiding beneath it to manipulate the device.

As for those gathered around the table, with the daylight flooding through the window, everyone's hands were in plain view. Besides, everyone's expression was rapt with unquestioning belief. Madam Saint Cloud was so busy with her pencil and paper that he couldn't imagine how she could be doing anything else.

The hand spun around in a final circle, and the arm underlined the single word 'done'. Those seated around the table leaned back in their chairs. The white-haired woman cleared her throat and looked down at what she had written. She began to read.

'The Indians cannot be trusted. Those who died at their hands know this above all else. They must be driven out before the orgy of slaughter. Blood will flow through the streets of London if they ride. None will be safe, not even the queen.'

That struck David as uncommonly specific for a communication from the great beyond. Of course, he only knew what he read in the newspapers, whenever the Society for Psychical Research exposed a fraudulent medium. Even so, he rather thought that so-called spirit guides sent messages so vague that anyone could read whatever meaning they wanted into them.

But he could see everyone around the table was convinced by this dire prediction. They were horrified, but he also realised, they weren't surprised. David guessed they had received similar messages before. But what was this particular group being warned about, and why now?

The butcher shook his head. 'I wrote to The Times. I told 'em. There's no call to have Indian cavalry in the procession, not when our brave boys are ready and willing to march to serve our queen.'

'It's a disgrace,' the tradeswoman said, shrill. 'I wrote to the Council. I said, no respectable woman will be safe with the likes of them roaming the streets.'

Her daughter nodded. 'We tell everyone who comes in the shop.'

'I spoke to my employer.' Gerald the clerk didn't elaborate. He simply shook his head, his face mournful.

'Adelaide,' Sergeant Shaw said suddenly. 'Is she – are you still there, Miss?'

David saw that interruption took Madam Saint Cloud by surprise. He hastily focused his attention on the psychic telegraph's dial, along with everyone else. The hand was motionless. Then the arm quivered. It spun around to underline the word 'Yes'.

'Is there any other threat?' Shaw gestured towards David. 'My friend here, can you see him? He was attacked –'

He broke off as the telegraph hand started spinning. This time it whirled around for several minutes. Everyone sat in rapt silence. Madam Saint Cloud looked as expectant as anyone else. This time, when the hand stopped, the group let Sergeant Shaw read the reply.

'Yes.'

He spelled out the short message that followed.

'I – S – E – E – H – I – M.'

It took every shred of David's resolve not to look around for whoever might be spying on them. Was there a peephole in the ceiling? Someone in a house opposite with a telescope trained on the uncurtained window? Though that didn't explain how they could hear what was being said.

The telegraph hand was moving again. This time, like before, everyone tried to guess the words to come. Finally the white-haired woman read the message in its entirety.

'The black men are the Indians' allies. Beware, beware the Bight of Benin.'

Everyone around the table chorused the rest of that well-known warning against having any dealings with the Dark Continent. 'For few come out though many go in.'

'What's that got to do with the price of fish?' The older maid was bemused.

'Adelaide? Adelaide? Are you still there?' Madam Saint Cloud asked, as if the other woman hadn't spoken.

The telegraph's hand stayed obstinately still.

The maid to David's right reached out to her neighbours with both hands. 'Shall we see who else –?'

'Not this afternoon, dear.' Madam Saint Cloud got to her feet. 'I think that's all for today.'

As the white-haired woman looked around the table, expectant, everyone rose from their seats, unprotesting. Even so, David could see they were variously surprised, disappointed or confused. Everyone except Sergeant Shaw. Once again, he was lost in thought.

David left the house with the others. He didn't say anything as he walked at the sergeant's side as they headed back to the tenement. When they reached the street corner, Shaw halted. He turned to David. Fury twisted his face.

'I knew it. I bloody knew it. When we saw them ready to fight for the Lescars. They're all in it together, the filth.'

'Who are, Sarge?' David tried to cut short another tirade. 'All together in what?'

Shaw chewed his lip, still red-faced with anger. 'You know the Jubilee Parade? You know the Indian Cavalry is going to take part? Well, what no one knows but us is those bastards are going to turn on the crowd. Cut down everyone they can reach. That's right, and they'll attack the royal visitors in their coaches too. Half the crowned 'eads of Europe will likely roll before the Life Guards and the Grenadiers will be able stop them. Adelaide's been warning us for weeks.'

'What?' David stared at Shaw in utter disbelief.

'It'll be a massacre, you mark my words.' The sergeant was so wrapped up in his fears that he took the young constable's incredulity for horror at the prospect. 'We have to show everyone they're not to be trusted, before it's too late.'

'So – the other night –' David hastily swallowed his words.

Shaw nodded regardless. 'We thought, me and a few others in the know, we thought if there was a riot that showed up the vicious bastards for the bloodthirsty savages they are, the Jubilee authorities would 'ave to think again.' He gave a hollow laugh. 'I can't 'ardly tell the Superintendent what I know and where that's come from. I'd be locked up in Colney 'atch for a lunatic, and what'd become of my Betsy then?'

He started walking again. 'But now we know it's even worse than we feared. It's not just the Indians acting alone. That beating you took weren't no coincidence. The Chinamen must be in on it and all.'

They walked back to the tenement. David did his best to ignore the sergeant's ceaseless condemnation of anyone who wasn't a true-born Englishman, coupled with spitting outrage at the sheer ingratitude of the Empire's subject races, when they should be giving thanks for blessings that ranged from railways to tea plantations.

Shaw had thankfully run out of invective by the time they got back. The sergeant disappeared into the room he shared with his wife. David went into the kitchen in search of a cup of tea, but he could see the strain on Mrs Shaw's face, when she asked where they had been.

'To see a lady, Mrs Saint Cloud –'

'She's no lady. She's a leech.' For all her anger, Mrs Shaw's eyes filled with tears. 'Whoever you've lost, young Davey, you mourn them decent and you let them go. That's what the good book says.'

Before he could find an answer, she turned away to busy herself at the sink. He could hear her sniffing, and saw her dab at her eyes with the hem of her apron.

David went to his room and lay down to try to get a little more sleep. That was a vain hope. Everything he had seen and heard whirled around in his head like a magic lantern show. However hard he tried, he couldn't make any sense of this bizarre business.

By the time the day shift began arriving back, David was already in his uniform. He had heard the sergeant leave a little while earlier, but had decided against walking to the station with him. For one thing, he didn't think he could stomach any more of Shaw's ranting today. Though he felt more sorry for the sergeant than anything else. David's anger was reserved for those unseen villains who were manipulating the man by playing on his grief. But the constable still could not work out how they had operated that infernal psychic telegraph.

Ralph opened the door. 'Wake up Dav– bloody 'ell, what happened to you?'

'Didn't duck fast enough. Mind out of the way.' He left the room, giving the same answer to the other constables.

David had time in hand before he was due on parade, as intended. Before he reached the station, he turned down a side street. On reaching the address he had memorised, he found a vacant shop front. He tried the handle and found the door was unlocked. On the mat he found a box, as promised. He opened it and found a mechanical rat, with its key lying beside it.

David wound the clockwork mechanism carefully, just as he had been shown. Thankfully the key went in the artificial creature's mouth rather than up its – rather than anywhere else. He held the rat by his side as he went out into the street again and closed the door behind him. The princess had assured him the entrance would be relocked before this beat's constable had a chance to check it.

There was no one in the street, so David put the creature down. As soon as its weight settled on its four little feet, the rat scurried off with its pre-prepared message that the constable had news. He watched it go and felt a ferocious urge to follow. No amount of clockwork was going to take it all the way to Richmond, he knew that much for a certainty. So was the rat heading for a station on the princess's private telegraph network? Who might be manning that?

He fought the temptation. Abidugun Sangodele had explained in no uncertain terms that they used the rats and other means of communication to keep everyone safe. David didn't need to know who the rat was going to, any more than whoever received it needed to know anything about the constable. What someone didn't know, they couldn't let slip, whether by accident or because the authorities were asking awkward questions. The authorities who would be more than ready to try a beating if that was what it took to get answers.

The rat was soon out of sight. David turned his back and headed for the station and his regular patrol. The night passed without much incident, certainly nothing out of the ordinary. He was on his way back to the station to report at the end of his shift, when he heard carriage wheels. A growler drew up beside him.

'Constable Price?' The driver looked down at him.

David didn't recognise the man, but Mr Sangodele opened the carriage door and beckoned to him.

'Get in.'

David quickly checked that there was no one to see him climb into the carriage. He would have to think of some excuse if anyone asked what he was doing when he stepped out again.

'Good morning, Constable Price.' The princess greeted him.

David guessed this four-seater was her personal carriage, for all that it looked like any other battered conveyance for hire rattling around London's streets. Inside, the predawn light was enough for him to see the floor and the velvet upholstery were spotless. This growler was a far cry from the grimy vehicles that delivered families with loads of luggage to the railway stations.

She wasted no time. 'You have news for us?'

'Er, yes.' David was momentarily distracted as Mr Sangodele reached up to thump the carriage roof with his cane. The growler pulled away. Well, that would draw less attention than the vehicle standing stationary on the street.

'Sergeant Shaw took me to a séance.' He explained everything that had happened in the purple-draped room.

Mr Sangodele took a notebook and a pencil from an inside pocket and began writing down the details. The princess listened intently, her eyes fixed on David's face.

'There is no such murderous conspiracy,' she insisted as he fell silent. 'You must believe that. These are lies spread by someone who hopes to benefit from stirring up mistrust of the Indian princely states. There's a long and sorry history of Imperial plundering based on flimsy excuses.'

'I know there can't be any such plan. It would be suicide for a start, and in any case, there'd be no keeping some scheme like that a secret.' He waved that away. 'But someone wants the Indian Cavalry out of the Jubilee procession. If we can work out how that trick with the psychic telegraph is worked, that might tell us who's trying to stir up this trouble. When we know who, that might tell us why.' He shook his head, frustrated. 'But I can't see for the life of me how they were doing it.'

Mr Sangodele and the princess shared a glance.

'Herzian waves?' he suggested.

'Perhaps.' She pursed her lips.

'What?' David demanded. 'Do you know the trick of it?'

'We might make a few guesses,' Mr Sangodele answered him.

'Unless there's no trick at all,' the princess countered. 'If someone has managed to communicate with the dead, there's no saying they couldn't enlist those with a lasting grudge against my people.'

David was nearly startled into a laugh. Then he realised she was wholly serious. His face must have given him away all the same.

The princess looked severely at him. 'There are more things in heaven and earth, Constable, than are dreamed of in your philosophy. The analytical engine sometimes tells us things even though no questions have been asked of it. We have no idea where those messages come from. Our ancestors perhaps?'

David had no idea how to answer her. To his relief, Mr Sangodele tapped his notebook with his pencil.

'We may well learn something useful if I make enquiries into this Madam Saint Cloud.'

'Establishing whose name is on the deed of that house for a start,' the princess agreed. She looked at David. 'We will be in touch as soon as we have news.'

'Meantime, don't arouse anyone's suspicions. Don't come to the princess's house again.' Mr Sangodele used his cane to tell the driver to stop.

The growler slowed and halted. David got out and looked warily around. He couldn't see anyone he knew on the street. He watched the carriage go, and wondered if it was headed to Richmond or somewhere else. He wondered if he would ever find out, or if he had served his purpose as far as these people were concerned.

FOUR

He'd heard nothing by the end of the week. He tried not to take that personally. Even with the princess's name and fortune to call on, making these enquiries must take time. Then who knew what fresh questions might have arisen from the answers that Mr Sangodele had initially found? If he could get answers, of course, If the colour of his skin wasn't seeing doors shut in his face, even with the princess's calling card in his hand.

The thing was, though, David was hearing more rumours of unease in the district, of suspicions directed at the Lascars, the Chinese and pretty much anyone who had come from overseas. No more than rumours and suspicion to be fair, nothing more than 'someone was telling me that someone they know...'. There were no actual crimes recorded, just gossip among the constables on their breaks in the day room or tales told by miscreants in the cells. He'd bet a fair few of these stories could be traced back to the people who had been sat around Madam Saint Cloud's table.

He tried not to fret about the Jubilee Procession, though the celebrations were getting ever closer. David guessed that the mysterious Adelaide's dire warnings were still coming, though he hadn't been invited to another séance. Sergeant Shaw was growing ever more tetchy, leaving the tenement in his off-duty hours while his wife grew increasingly unhappy.

The constable wished there was some way to put an end to Madam Saint Cloud's goings-on, but he couldn't think what to do. If he went to his own inspector, the first person the station's superior officer would ask about the woman would be the sergeant. That would tell Shaw he had been betrayed and that would be the end of David's chances of learning anything else that the princess needed to know. It was also a fair bet that the sergeant would convince the inspector to dismiss any thought of investigating. He might even tell Madam Saint Cloud something that risked word getting back to whoever was behind her. That would put the scoundrels on notice that their schemes had been discovered.

By Monday morning, David had had enough of these thoughts swirling around in his head like a dog chasing its tail. It was all very well the princess and Mr Sangodele telling him to leave investigating these matters to them, but when it came down to it, for all their wealth and connections, they were foreigners. They certainly weren't part of the Metropolitan Police, and his superiors had a right to know about this threat to the rule of law and good order.

After his shift was over, he didn't go back to the tenement. Instead he headed for the district headquarters, still wearing his uniform. No one questioned his right to be there as he went up the steps and in through the station's doors. The layout inside was unfamiliar, but he found the day room easily enough. A burly sergeant whom David didn't recognise was entering a report in the ledger. His lips were moving under his moustache as he painstakingly wrote a fair copy of the notes he had made in his occurrence book.

Hearing boots, the sergeant glanced up and looked mildly surprised to see a stranger. 'What can I do for you, Constable?'

'Constable David Price, Sarge.' He stood smartly to attention. 'Would it be possible to see Superintendent Hudson?'

The superintendent was the highest ranked officer David had ever had dealings with, even if that only amounted to fetching him a cup of tea when he visited their station to confer with their inspector about concerns well above David's rank. He held his breath. If the superintendent wasn't here, he would have to ask who the highest ranking officer currently in the headquarters might be. That would undoubtedly prompt questions from this sharp-eyed sergeant which David would really prefer not to answer.

The sergeant laid down his pen. 'He's here, but he'll want to know what this is about.'

'It's a sensitive matter,' David said resolutely.

'Is that so?' The sergeant studied him for a long moment. Then he shrugged. 'On your head be it. Wait here.'

He left the day room for a corridor that David guessed led to the cells from the noise. He heard the sergeant knock on a door, but he couldn't make out what was said thanks to someone sobbing, and a shrewish tirade of foul insults being yelled at every and any policeman.

'You shut your racket,' the sergeant shouted over his shoulder as he returned. He nodded at David. 'He'll see you. Third door on the left.'

'Thank you, Sarge.' David's momentary elation was swiftly replaced by nervousness as he approached the superintendent's door. He raised his shaking hand and accidentally knocked harder than he had intended.

'Come in.' The superintendent looked at David with frank curiosity as he entered. 'So what brings you here? Something that you can't tell my sergeant about, and which you see fit not to share with your own superiors? You had better not be wasting my time.' His tone was chillingly cold.

'Sir.' David swallowed hard as he took off his helmet and tucked it under his arm. He stood to attention in front of the superintendent's vast and cluttered desk. 'I don't want them to think I'm a fool, sir. I think there's something smoky going on, but it sounds like a fanciful tale from some penny paper. If I'm wrong, I'll never hear the last of it.'

He had spent restless days in his cramped room, as well as the nights pounding his beat, racking his brains for some justification for going outside his chain of command. This was paper-thin, but it was the best he had come up with. It might well do his prospects no good at all, but he could always transfer to another district or even to another force if worst came to worst.

What he wouldn't do – what he couldn't do – was betray Sergeant Shaw's involvement in what he was about to say. Not and see the sergeant's reputation ruined and his pension lost, with him and his poor wife turned out of their home. No one in their station would ever forgive David for that. He would never forgive himself.

'There's a spiritualist lady on our patch, sir, holds séances and the like. Madam Saint Cloud she calls herself. The thing is, she's stirring up trouble from what I hear. Prejudicial to good order and liable to cause a breach of the peace sooner or later. Accusing foreign sorts she doesn't like the look of, saying they're not loyal to our queen.'

'That sounds unpleasant, but it's hardly actionable, Constable,' the superintendent said severely. 'I thought you were coming to me about corruption or some such.'

'No, sir. Sorry, sir.' As much as David wished the floor would open up and swallow him, he stood his ground. 'She's done nothing that I can officially take notice of, but she's stringing grieving people along, playing on their losses – from what I hear. She might well convince someone to do something rash, something criminal, while she keeps her sly hands clean. It's just not right, sir.' He couldn't hold back his anger as he thought of the cruel way Sergeant Shaw was being duped.

Superintendent Hudson was evidently taken aback by his passion. He leaned forward, resting his elbows on the desk. 'What do you expect me to do about this, Constable?'

David was heartened to see that was a genuine question, not a rebuke. 'See what the detective branch can find out about her, sir? Find out what her real name might be? See if another force knows her for a fraud?'

The superintendent looked thoughtful. 'It would hardly be the first time one of these charlatans has fled their crimes in provinces to hide in the capital.'

'Exactly so, sir.' David breathed a discreet sigh of relief.

Hudson rose and gestured to an upright wooden chair for visitors. 'Take a seat. I'd like you to write this down, everything that you know or suspect. Let me find some paper.'

David pulled the chair up to the edge of the desk and got his pencil out of his pocket. The superintendent was opening a drawer in a cabinet behind him.

'Do you –?'

He had barely started to turn when something hard struck him solidly behind the ear. David felt his forehead hit the desk. Then he knew no more.

He had the most godawful headache, and he felt horribly sick. David felt panic rising with his nausea as he realised there was a gag in his mouth. He swallowed the urge to vomit. What might happen if he spewed didn't bear thinking about.

As he drew deep breaths in through his nose, the crisis passed. Now David realised his hands and feet were bound. He was lying on a floor, he realised next. He opened his eyes, and immediately closed them as he felt dizzy and sick once again. He took a few more deep breaths. That headache really was villainous. What on Earth had happened?

He heard a handle and the sweep of a door brushing over a thick carpet. He opened his eyes, more cautiously this time. He could see the back and legs of a chair upholstered with fine green leather and the carved wooden moulding of a library's bottom shelves. Then he heard voices.

'Where is he?'

'Over in the corner. He's still out for the count.'

David closed his eyes and lay as limp as he could, in case one of them came over to make sure that was true. He couldn't hear their footsteps on this carpeted floor.

'Keep him somewhere until midnight, then cosh him again and throw him in the river.' The first speaker was unconcerned.

'You don't think we should see what else he knows? Who else he might have told?'

Sluggish outrage burned through the fog of David's headache as he recognised the second voice. That was Superintendent Hudson. Slowly, piece by piece, he began to recall what had happened to him. Then he realised the first man was talking again. He forced himself to concentrate.

'– end of her usefulness. We don't have the time to waste stirring up trouble around the docks any more. I've said from the start that we need to take far more decisive action.' The aristocratic voice grew harsh with anger. 'It's a damn outrage. What sap decided that Indians should play such a prominent part in the Jubilee Procession? I hear they've even convinced the queen to take some of them into her household. Can you believe it? They say that foul muck they call curry has been served at her table.'

He couldn't have been more furious if he was saying the queen had been served roast dog. The voice broke off. David heard a clink of crystal and the slosh of liquid before something was set down on a metal tray. He realised he was desperately thirsty.

The first man spoke again, less angry than before but just as resolute. 'These fools who don't think twice about trusting their inferiors, they have no idea what they are doing. These shows of favour will make it harder than ever to keep the natives in their place, and not just in India. It's time to put an end to this nonsense once and for all.'

'I agree,' Superintendent Hudson said, exasperated. 'But how?'

The first voice laughed with a callousness that sent a chill down David's spine.

'We plant a bomb at the Indian Cavalry barracks. The bastards can't ride in the Jubilee parade if half of them are dead or injured.'

'A bomb?' Superintendent Hudson was startled. 'No, absolutely not. Such a loss of life, even Indian lives, will cast a pall over the whole Jubilee. We cannot do that to her majesty. You know what a soft heart she has.'

The callous man hissed through his teeth. 'I suppose so. Very well. We will bring down a section of the outer wall, maybe a few buildings. That will give them plenty to fuss over.'

'You must make certain the stables aren't damaged,' Hudson warned.

'What do you take me for?' The first voice was outraged. 'I won't see a hair on any horse hurt.'

'I should hope not.' Hudson clearly still had his reservations. 'But even without bloodshed, something so dramatic will prompt a major investigation. We can delay things and mislay evidence, but we won't be able to shut the enquiries down completely.'

'You won't need to.' The first voice was unconcerned. 'We will supply whatever evidence you need. It's only been a couple of years since the last Fenian bombings. We can easily make sure the Irish get the blame.'

'Will that really serve our purposes?' Hudson remained to be convinced.

'As far as the public are concerned. As for these jumped-up colonial types, we can make sure they realise that anyone stepping out of line will get more of the same.' The first voice laughed, as heartless as before. 'Who are they going to tell? Who would ever believe them?'

'So when are we doing this?' Hudson seemed to have set aside his doubts.

'As soon as possible,' the first man said briskly. 'No time like the present.'

David heard what he guessed was the clunk of a brandy glass or some such being set down.

The callous man laughed for a third and final time. 'And no one will be grieving over some constable who got himself knocked on the head and thrown in the river if they're busy chasing after Fenians.'

David heard the door open and close. As soon as he heard the key turn in the lock, he began fighting against his bonds. He tried and tried until he lost track of time. He lay there, exhausted and with his head spinning. It was no use. The finest rope that some chandler's on the docks could supply had been knotted around his wrists and ankles.

Not that these bonds would leave a mark, he realised some while later. He wriggled and looked down at his hands tied in front of his belt buckle. The rope had been wrapped around the cuffs of his uniform, tight enough to hold him but loose enough not to dig in. The same was true of the rope around his sturdy leather boots. There would be nothing to arouse suspicion when his corpse was fished out of the Thames.

David tried to fight rising panic, but his breaths came shorter and faster. He started to feel sick again, and this time the nausea was worse. He tried to twist his face to the floor, terrified that he would choke to death if he vomited. Either that or he was about to suffer an apoplexy. He could feel his heart pounding in his chest hard enough to crack his ribs. His head was splitting.

The door handle rattled. David froze. He heard a muffled conversation, and then more rattling. A few moments later, the door opened. David drew up his knees and prepared to fight, to sell his life dear. He could kick and he could headbutt. Whatever these killers had to do to subdue him, he would leave his mark on the bastards.

An African appeared at the side of the leather upholstered chair. 'Abidugun!'

Mr Sangodele joined him. 'Constable Price.' His relief was palpable.

David closed his eyes and went limp. He gave silent thanks to his guardian angel or whatever earthly power had sent this rescue.

'Lie still.' The unknown African produced a workman's knife from his coat pocket and carefully cut through the linen cloth gagging David. He swiftly sliced his rope bonds. 'Can you stand? Can you walk?'

'I think so.' David struggled to his hands and knees. 'I —'

He twisted and managed not to vomit on Mr Sangodele. The tall man sprang back regardless, and looked over his shoulder. He said something in an unknown tongue. By the time David had finished being profoundly sick, the unknown African gentleman was offering him a crystal tumbler half-filled with what proved to be brandy.

Still kneeling, David took a mouthful, swilled it around, and spat the foulness onto the floor. He felt a momentary pang for the maid who'd have to clean up the horrid mess, but that couldn't be helped. 'Listen —'

'Let's get you out of here.' Mr Sangodele stooped to help him to his feet.

'Listen to me!' David pulled his arm free. 'There's going to be a bomb set at the Indian Cavalry barracks.'

He wiped his mouth with the linen that had been used to gag him, and told them what he had heard. Unsurprisingly, both men were appalled. David expected at least one of them to go rushing off. Instead, Mr Sangodele produced what looked like a pocket book made of brass from an inner pocket of his coat. He went to stand by the window and opened it. David couldn't see what he was doing, but he heard an uneven series of rapid clicks.

He looked at his other rescuer. 'What is that?'

'Wireless telegraph.' The African gentleman grinned. 'Using Herzian waves.'

That meant nothing to David, but he guessed this was yet another invention funded by the princess.

Mr Sangodele closed the device. 'The necessary steps will be taken.'

'What steps?' demanded David. 'Have you alerted the authorities? The police?'

'The authorities? The police?' Mr Sangodele gesture took in the library and the house beyond it. 'Where do you think you are? Who do you think brought you here?'

'We must leave,' the other African said urgently. 'Now.'

This time David didn't resist. He drank the rest of the brandy, and allowed them both to help him to his feet. The three men headed for the library door.

'Wait!' David saw his helmet, truncheon, lantern and whistle sitting on a table. He snatched everything up. 'Right. Let's go.'

Out in the hallway there was no sign of any servants. The house's main door stood ajar. David followed Mr Sangodele out into a square of elegant, identical white-painted houses. This must be one of London's wealthier quarters, but he couldn't guess at more than that. His head was still aching and now he grew dizzy. Thankfully he only had to cross a narrow stretch of pavement to reach the waiting growler.

He was relieved to find this was a far more workaday vehicle than the princess's conveyance. Better yet, the air in this prosperous part of London was clean enough to help clear his head a little. Both the other men got in after him and Mr Sangodele closed the carriage door. The driver whipped up the horse without any need for instruction.

David leaned back in the seat and closed his eyes. 'How did you find me?'

Mr Sangodele answered him. 'The analytical engine.'

'What?' David opened his eyes. 'How?'

'Mrs Leigh asked the machine to predict your possible courses of action.' Mr Sangodele raised a hand. 'Please, do not ask me how. She said the chances were high that you would seek out Superintendent Hudson.'

'You were following me?' David didn't know whether to be outraged or relieved.

'You and him both.' Mr Sangodele was unrepentant. 'The analytical engine had already identified Hudson as a likely threat. But we had no idea that Sir George was involved,' he added thoughtfully.

David wanted to ask who Sir George was, when he was at home. He wanted to know how two Africans had forced their way into a knight of the realm's home, and where the servants had gone. But the energy that had propelled him out of that house was fading fast. Despite all his efforts, despite Mr Sangodele urging him to stay awake, he slipped into a swoon.

FIVE

This time he woke up in a bed. He could feel crisp white pillows against his face and a silken coverlet beneath his fingertips. Fresh flowers perfumed the air and gauzy drapes softened the daylight coming through the windows. David realised his head was no longer aching, but as he raised a cautious hand, he found a bandage swathing his crown. Looking at his arm, he saw he wore a fine cotton nightshirt.

'Would you like some water?' The dark-complexioned maid with the Whitechapel accent appeared at the foot of the bed.

She must have been sitting close by and seen him stir. David swallowed and found his mouth was stale and dry. 'Yes, please.'

The girl came over and raised his head with a gentle hand. She held a glass to his lips and David sipped water with a squeeze of lemon juice. He couldn't remember ever tasting something so wonderful. Then he realised he was fiercely hungry.

'What happened?' he asked as soon as the maid took the glass away. At least he didn't have to ask where he was.

'I'll tell madam that you're awake.' She disappeared before David could protest.

Cautiously, he sat up in the bed. Once it was apparent that the evil headache wasn't going to return, he surveyed his surroundings. The bedroom's walls were hung with elegant striped paper, and it was furnished with a mahogany tallboy and a wardrobe. There were two lightweight armchairs and a small table by the fireplace, and overall the room was more than twice the size of the one he shared in his lodgings.

As he thought that, he forgot about admiring the décor. This couldn't be the same day as he had been attacked, but how long had he lain there senseless? He ran a hand over his chin, but his skin was smooth. Someone had shaved him while he slept, and he realised, sponge-bathed him as well.

That was all very well and good, but how many days had he been absent without leave from his duties as a constable? How on earth was he ever going to explain himself? He looked around the room. Where was his uniform?

The door opened and the princess came in. She carried a leather document case, and she was smiling with evident satisfaction. 'Good morning, Constable.'

The maid brought over one of the chairs so that the princess could sit close to the head of the bed.

'Good morning, ma'am. Please,' David asked urgently. 'What day is this?'

'It's Wednesday. Mr Sangodele's brother is a doctor, and he deemed it wisest to keep you asleep for a period of recuperation once he was satisfied there was no need to treat your concussion with trephining. He is an excellent doctor,' she assured him.

'Thank you.' David had no idea what trephining might be, but he was glad to have escaped it. 'Please, where are my clothes? I have to —'

'We managed to foil the bomb plot. Indeed, thanks to you, we managed to do a great deal more.' She opened the document case and leaned forward to pass him a handful of photographs.

David sorted through the pictures. They were small as these things always were, not even three inches across, and for some reason, they were circular rather than square. No matter, the images were clear enough, especially once the princess passed him a magnifying glass. He saw a gang of men busy around a flat-bed cart that seemed to have lost a wheel. Its load of sacks had spilled out onto the road. Now a man was unharnessing the horse to lead it away. In the final photograph, the men were stacking the sacks against a wall, ostensibly out of the way of passing traffic.

David looked at the princess, incredulous. 'You set up a camera? A tripod and plates and everything?'

'Oh no, we have something far more discreet, sent from America by a friend who knows of my interest in scientific developments. A gentleman called George Eastman is working to perfect what he calls his Kodak camera. It's no more than six inches long.' She sketched a rough box shape in the air with her hands. 'It takes photographs at the press of a button and uses what they call a roll of film instead of glass plates. It's really quite marvellous, and I expect it will be all the rage when it goes on sale in a year or so.'

She handed him more photographs. David saw gloved hands removing the pile of sacks to reveal what could only be the bomb. He shivered at the thought of anyone taking such a risk.

'Thankfully one of our number has copious experience with explosives, after working in the mines of Southern Africa,' the princess said quietly. 'He was able to frustrate this vile threat, and we removed the device without anyone in the barracks being any the wiser.'

David looked up from the pictures. 'What are you going to do with it?'

'We have already rendered it useless,' she assured him. 'We are far more interested in identifying these men and establishing who gave them their orders.'

David chewed his lip. 'The superintendent...'

'I intend to show him these photographs,' the princess said brightly. 'This very afternoon. Would you please accompany me? Dr Sangodele's has given his permission.'

'Me?' David was startled.

'I will do all the talking,' the princess assured him. 'So, will you come?'

'I... Yes.' He couldn't see that he had any other option.

'Excellent.' The princess gathered up the photographs and the magnifying glass. 'Now, would you like something to eat?'

That at least was a simple question. 'Yes, please. Thank you.'

'I will have something sent up.' The princess departed without further ado.

That 'something' turned out to be a dish of spiced rice with smoked haddock flaked into it, dressed with parsley and chopped hard-boiled eggs. He contemplated it with some misgiving.

'Kedgeree.' The maid set the tray table on the bed across David's knees. 'You should try it.'

Since he was now utterly ravenous, he picked up the fork despite his misgivings. He was glad he did. With a full belly, he felt far more like himself. Better yet, while he was eating, the maid returned with his police uniform sponged clean and freshly pressed. Every button on his tunic had been polished. She laid everything on the end of the bed, along with a clean shirt, socks and drawers.

'Thank you,' David said awkwardly. 'I'm sorry, I don't know your name.'

She spared him a swift smile. 'You can call me Abi.'

He wondered if that was short for Abigail or some other outlandish name entirely. He decided not to ask. At soon as she left the room, David got out of the bed and went to look at his reflection in the mirror over the mantelpiece. He looked sallow and drawn, and the bandage around his head would draw all eyes. He found the knot securing it and picked that apart. Unwinding the bandage, he discovered a lint dressing towards the back of his head and above his right ear. David tested it with cautious fingertips. That particular area of his scalp had been shaved, and the dressing showed no inclination to come loose. There was a very tender spot underneath it so he decided to leave well alone.

He dressed quickly, and found that this shirt was not merely clean, it felt like it had never been worn. As for the drawers and socks, those were silk, and he really didn't know what to make of that.

He was fastening his collar when there was a knock at the door. 'Are you decent?'

He cleared his throat. 'Come in.'

Abi had brought his boots, polished to a high shine, together with his belt, helmet, truncheon, whistle and lamp. 'Madam's in the drawing room.'

'I'll be down directly.' He donned his helmet with considerable care, not wanting to dislodge that dressing.

Once he had his official accoutrements secured, David felt his resolve strengthen. He had done nothing wrong. If Superintendent Hudson thought he could discipline him for his absence, the man could damn well answer for his attack on him, superior officer or not. Once the princess had finished with the swine, of course.

He found the lady waiting in the hall when he went downstairs. Outside, a carriage was waiting, and this was no anonymous growler but the latest fashionable conveyance with the princess's coat of arms painted on the door. Built to accommodate gentlemen's silk hats, there was sufficient headroom for David to wear his helmet. The coachman had the lively pair of white horses well in hand, and the vehicle carried them smoothly away. Even with the usual bustle of traffic slowing them down as they crossed London, they arrived at the district headquarters in a fraction of the time that the journey would have taken by omnibus.

David got out, unfolded the carriage step, and held the door open. 'Your highness.'

'Thank you. Will you carry this for me?' She handed him the leather document case.

Today, the princess wore a light creamy wrap over a golden silk dress. Her straw bonnet was decorated with white and yellow feathers that came from no bird David could put a name to, and she carried a white silk parasol. David saw passers-by stopping to stare. This district was not used to visitors of this quality, whatever the colour of their skin.

The princess appeared not to notice this unabashed scrutiny. 'Where is the superintendent's office?' she asked him as he closed the carriage door.

'There's a corridor leads off the day room, off to the left. Third door on the left.'

She nodded. 'Lead on.'

David went up the station steps, doing his best to emulate the princess's poise. With him in uniform, nobody challenged their right to enter. So far, so good, but he knew the duty sergeant would be a different matter. He braced himself as they reached the day room.

The sergeant looked up from his mug of tea and was visibly startled to see such an exotic visitor. 'How can I –?'

The princess simply ignored him. She went down the corridor to the left. David hurried after her. He could hear the sergeant following them.

'Here, you can't –' Outraged, the man was lost for words as this imperious stranger threw open the superintendent's door without knocking.

Superintendent Hudson was sat at his desk. 'What the –?'

He looked up and David saw two things within the blink of an eye. First, Hudson's utter confusion as he looked at the princess. Secondly, the bastard's absolute horror as he recognised the young constable. The superintendent turned positively ashen.

'Now, you just wait a minute, Miss.' The duty sergeant came up behind them, wrathful.

'No, that's all right,' Hudson said quickly. 'I – oh, just shut the bloody door, man. Be off with you!'

The sergeant gaped and then retreated, as affronted as he was baffled

The princess sat demurely on the vacant chair, one white-gloved hand resting on her parasol and the other in her lap. 'Good afternoon, Superintendent Hudson.'

'Good afternoon,' he said awkwardly, 'but you have the advantage of me, madam. Might I know your name?'

Although Hudson was talking to the princess, his gaze had strayed to David who was standing at ease by the door. David made sure to keep his face impassive.

The princess ignored Hudson's question, turning in her seat instead. 'Constable, please show the superintendent our photographs.'

David advanced and opened the document case. As he handed over the pictures, one by one, he realised there were far more photographs here than the ones he had already seen. There were several of Superintendent Hudson walking or talking with an immaculately dressed gentleman in a tall silk hat. David guessed he was the cold-hearted swine who had plotted wholesale murder with such ease. Then the superintendent reached the series of photographs of the broken-down cart. His hands started shaking.

'I'm sure you and your friends have been wondering why your bomb didn't go off as planned. You must have been bitterly disappointed,' the princess said sweetly. 'Well, now you know.'

'You – I –' Hudson wrenched open a drawer in his desk and rummaged inside.

The princess took her parasol in both hands and twisted the handle. It came off and she pointed it at Hudson like a pistol. It must actually be a pistol, David realised a second later. He hadn't thought the superintendent could turn any paler, but somehow the man had managed it.

'Please, don't be so foolish,' the princess entreated him. 'Constable, kindly relieve Superintendent Hudson of his weapon.'

David put down the document case and went around the desk, careful not to obstruct the princess's shot. He found a Webley revolver in the drawer that Hudson had just opened. He retreated to the door with the weapon in his hand, and fervently prayed that he wouldn't have to use the thing.

'All right, let's have it,' Hudson snarled. 'What are you going to do? What have I got to do for you? Do you want money?'

'Oh, you need do nothing at all. In fact, we insist on it.' The princess looked up from securing the handle on her parasol once again. 'That's to say, you will withdraw from Sir George's circle and take no further part in his foul schemes. Naturally, you will not tell him why. In return, we will not send the considerable amount of evidence which we have gathered of your involvement in this attempted outrage to the Police Commissioner. Constable Price here will not go to see him accompanied by my personal solicitor, to present a sworn statement detailing your murderous assault on a junior officer and your willingness to see him later killed.'

She raised a hand as Hudson opened his mouth to protest. 'Finding some excuse to convince Sir George is a challenge you must meet without my assistance. Know this, you will be watched. If you do not do as we ask, I will have no option but to see you disgraced and prosecuted. Rest assured that I am not working alone. If anything untoward happens to me, my solicitor has copies of the relevant photographs and documents, as well as my instructions to reveal everything to the authorities and to the newspapers. So do other trusted friends whom you will not be able to identify, I assure you. The same applies to Constable Price. If he suffers any injury or retaliation, I will see that you are held accountable, to the fullest extent of the law.'

David wondered how these calm words could sound quite so menacing, delivered in the princess's cut-glass accents as she sat there dressed in the height of fashion, so slender and of such modest height. Then he concentrated on looking as if he had known what she was going to say all along.

'Do I have your word?' The princess rose to her feet.

Hudson was staring at the photographs like a man gazing into hell. He looked up. 'What? Yes, damn your eyes. I swear it.'

'Excellent.' The princess swept the photographs deftly together and put them back in the document case. She glanced over her shoulder. 'Return the superintendent's weapon, Constable.'

'Ma'am?' David was startled. On the other hand... He had been wondering how he would get out of the station unchallenged, if he was still holding the gun.

He studied the thing and found a lever on the side, just in front of the handle. He pushed it and the muzzle dropped down a fraction. He realised that the weapon was designed to break open much in the manner of a shotgun. He opened it and swallowed an oath as a rod tipped with a star-shaped piece of metal emerged from the centre of the cylinder. That scattered the bullets over the floor.

Well, he had wanted to unload it, so that was good enough. Hudson doubtless had more ammunition in his drawer, but they would be gone before the villain could find it. He would have to pursue them, and the superintendent would hardly shoot them in front of witnesses, would he?

David tossed the gun onto the desk. It landed with a thud, but Hudson barely reacted. He was sitting with his head in his hands, staring down at nothing at all.

'Let's go. Close the door behind us.' The princess was already leaving.

David followed her. Out in the corridor, the affronted sergeant was blocking their way to the day room.

'Now you look here, Miss,' he began.

The gunshot was shockingly loud. The sergeant stood open-mouthed for a moment, blank-faced with incomprehension. Then he hurried down the corridor, shoving David out of his way.

The young constable followed the princess as she headed in the other direction. She hitched up the hem of her dress, and was showing a remarkable turn of speed in her cream kidskin button boots. Behind them, the sergeant was shouting. David couldn't make out his words. Other voices joined the hubbub as every man in the station was drawn to this unforseen crisis.

No one thought to stop them leaving. David had no idea why, and he wasn't about to ask. They reached the sanctuary of the princess's carriage. The driver urged the horses into a smart trot before David had secured the latch on the door. Once he had done that, he sat down on the seat opposite the princess and stared dumbly at her. For the first time in their brief acquaintance, her self-possession faltered.

'The analytical engine did calculate that was one possible outcome. I had no idea he would do such a desperate thing so swiftly.' Then she rallied, lifting her chin. 'We are relieved of one enemy at least.'

David couldn't believe what he was hearing. 'You knew he was going to kill himself? Why, that's – *this* – it's as good as –' He choked on the word 'murder'.

'We did not know,' the princess retorted. 'We can never be certain. We can only balance probabilities, and try to chart our best course through the options they present.'

David shook his head. 'What am I supposed to say when I'm asked what happened? When I'm asked what business I had there?'

'You say that you have no idea why he did such a dreadful thing. You say that we had already left his office,' the princess said forcefully. 'If you are asked anything at all.'

David persisted. 'My superiors will want to know why I was there in the first place.'

'I very much doubt it. Bear in mind that you were knocked senseless in that very station,' the princess pointed out. 'Somehow you were carried unconscious to Sir George's house. Superintendent Hudson cannot have done that alone. Whoever else was involved will hardly want such a shady business dragged into the light.'

David opened his mouth and then closed it again. 'I still have to account for my absence to Sergeant Shaw.'

'Dr Sangodele will say you were brought to his charity hospital unconscious. It wasn't until you recovered today that you could identify yourself. Then they realised that your uniform had been found dumped close by. Since you have no idea who attacked you, what precisely occurred will remain a mystery,' she said blandly.

David wondered what Mrs Williams at the chapel back home would have to say about telling such lies, even in the service of a good cause. He also noted the ease with which the princess concocted such falsehoods. He wondered what she might have told him that wasn't entirely true.

'You will need to consider your future prospects as a policeman, though.' The princess managed to be somehow sympathetic and unyielding at the same time. 'Your name is undoubtedly known to those who conspired with Superintendent Hudson. I meant what I said when I warned him to leave you alone, but he killed himself before he could communicate that to his allies. We will ensure the same message reaches Sir George, but there is no knowing if he will comply. There are far too many ways to contrive what would appear to be some regrettably fatal accident for a constable.'

David remembered the bastard's callous laugh in the library. 'He will want revenge. He was ready to see me dead before you wrecked his plans.' His voice shook.

'This is a matter of life and death for us all,' the princess said with sudden passion, 'and for countless thousands beyond these shores.'

David swallowed an urge to say that was all very well, but he hadn't asked to be dragged into this business. But that wasn't quite true, was it? He could have looked the other way, and taken different paths several times to avoid ending up here in this carriage with this princess. Now he was in this fix, what was he going to do? Run away like some coward?

He took his truncheon out of its pocket and traced the painted division letter and his warrant number with a thoughtful finger. 'What would I do to earn my crust, if I resign from the police?'

'I will find you employment,' the princess promised.

He looked up. 'Do you have another ally who's a serving officer?'

The princess hesitated.

'You don't, do you?' David looked back at his truncheon again.

'You need not make any hasty decisions.' The princess gazed out of the carriage window. 'You must forgive me, I have a final fitting at my dressmaker's. I dine at Windsor in a few days. Donaldson will take you back to the house. We can discuss this further when I return.'

David resisted the temptation to point out that he didn't take orders from her. She seemed content to take his silence for agreement. Neither of them said a word as the carriage wound its way through London. The princess was delivered to her dressmaker and David was conveyed in comfort to Richmond. The maid Abi answered the front door to his knock.

'Oh, you're back.' She seemed pleased to see him which was a welcome surprise.

'The princess – we're to talk when she gets back from her fitting,' he explained awkwardly.

'You can wait in the drawing room.' Abi led the way. 'Can I get you anything? Tea? A newspaper, perhaps?'

'Thank you.' David wasn't entirely sure which question he was answering.

As it turned out, Abi brought him both. David drank several much-needed cups of tea as he read the reports of the viewing stands and other temporary buildings that dozens of carpenters were erecting by Westminster Abbey. He marvelled at the prices that shops and other businesses along the procession's route were charging for tickets to a seat in their windows or even up on their roof, to see the queen and the visiting dignitaries go by.

Then he folded the newspaper and left the drawing room. He walked the short distance up the hall and stopped outside the room that was so much more than a library. Taking a deep breath, he knocked on the door.

A female voice answered. 'Come in?'

David opened the door and was surprised to find the room empty today, apart from a young Chinese lady. She sat at the table beside the analytical engine, where she was selecting punched cards from different trays to make a stack that she kept secure with a vulcanised India rubber band.

She looked at him with mild enquiry. 'Can I help you with something?'

David remembered a story from school about Julius Caesar crossing a river called the Rubicon. He stepped into the room. 'I hope so, Miss – Miss?'

'Miss Lam.' She continued with her mysterious work.

David studied the analytical engine, taking in every detail this time. Now he noticed several white enamelled dials amid its complexities. While these didn't resemble the psychic telegraph beyond being circular with an indicating hand, he was reminded of Madam Saint Cloud's séance. Was he willing to trust his future to guidance from an equally inexplicable source?

He looked at Miss Lam. 'Do you know how to ask this engine to predict the likely outcomes of different courses of action? Of different choices that I might make?'

Queen Victoria's glorious Golden Jubilee procession passed off without incident on 21ˢᵗ June 1887. Newly transferred to the Westminster division, Constable David Price was among the policemen keeping the joyful populace in check as they marvelled at the spectacle. The Indian Cavalry escorting her majesty were much admired and loudly cheered.

As the long summer twilight faded into a luminous night, the crowds outside Buckingham Palace admired the largest ever display of fireworks that London had ever seen, devised to entertain her majesty's numerous royal and titled guests after their sumptuous banquet.

Constable Price was not among the throng as they oohed and aahed. He was on his way to Richmond.

ABOUT THE AUTHOR

Juliet E McKenna is a British fantasy author living in the Cotswolds, UK. Loving history, myth and other worlds since she first learned to read, she has written fifteen epic fantasy novels so far. Her debut, *The Thief's Gamble*, began The Tales of Einarinn in 1999, followed by The Aldabreshin Compass sequence, The Chronicles of the Lescari Revolution, and The Hadrumal Crisis trilogy. *The Green Man's Heir* was her first modern fantasy rooted in British folklore in 2018, followed by *The Green Man's Foe, The Green Man's Silence*, and *The Green Man's Challenge*. She writes and comments on book trade issues, has served as a judge for major genre awards, and reviews online and for magazines. She writes diverse short stories and novellas enjoying forays into darker fantasy, steampunk and SF. She has also written murder mysteries set in ancient Greece as J M Alvey.

Also from NewCon Press

Steampunk International edited by Ian Whates

English language edition of an anthology showcasing the very best Steampunk stories from three different countries: UK, Finland, and Italy; released by three different publishers in three different languages. UK contributors are George Mann (an original Newbury and Hobbes tale), Jonathan Green, Derry O'Dowd.

Night, Rain, and Neon edited by Michael Cobley

All new cyberpunk stories from Ian McDonald, Louise Carey, Jon Courtenay Grimwood, Justina Robson, Simon Morden, Gary Gibson, DA Xiaolin Spires, Al Robertson, Keith Brooke & Eric Brown, T.R. Napper, Jeremy Szal, Gavin Smith, Tim Maughan, Stewart Hotston and more.

Queen of Clouds – Neil Williamson

Wooden automata, sentient weather, talking cats, compellant inks and a host of vividly realised characters provide the backdrop to this rich dark fantasy, as stranger in the city Billy Braid becomes embroiled in Machiavellian politics and deadly intrigue.

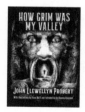

How Grim Was My Valley – John Llewellyn Probert

Robert wakes up on the Severn Bridge with no memory of who he is. He embarks on an odyssey through Wales, bearing witness to the stories both the people and the land itself feel moved to tell him, on a quest to discover the truth of his identity, wherever that may lead.

The Queen of Summer's Twilight – Charles Vess

A mysterious man on a black motorbike rescues a rebellious teen from the streets of Inverness, setting in motion a series of events that will see contemporary Scotland clash with the realm of fairy, in this stunning tale inspired by the ballad of Tam Lyn.

www.newconpress.co.uk

Ingram Content Group UK Ltd.
Milton Keynes UK
UKHW011811060423
419751UK00004B/229